for keeps

Natasha Friend

speak

An Imprint of Penguin Group (USA) Inc.

SPEAK
Published by the Penguin Group
Penguin Group (USA) Inc., 345 Hudson Street, New York, New York 10014, U.S.A.
Penguin Group (Canada), 90 Eglinton Avenue East, Suite 700, Toronto, Ontario, Canada M4P 2Y3
(a division of Pearson Penguin Canada Inc.)
Penguin Books Ltd, 80 Strand, London WC2R 0RL, England
Penguin Ireland, 25 St Stephen's Green, Dublin 2, Ireland (a division of Penguin Books Ltd)
Penguin Group (Australia), 250 Camberwell Road, Camberwell, Victoria 3124, Australia
(a division of Pearson Australia Group Pty Ltd)
Penguin Books India Pvt Ltd, 11 Community Centre, Panchsheel Park, New Delhi - 110 017, India
Penguin Group (NZ), 67 Apollo Drive, Rosedale, Auckland 0632, New Zealand
(a division of Pearson New Zealand Ltd)
Penguin Books (South Africa) (Pty) Ltd, 24 Sturdee Avenue,
Rosebank, Johannesburg 2196, South Africa

Registered Offices: Penguin Books Ltd, 80 Strand, London WC2R 0RL, England

First published in the United States of America by Viking, a member of Penguin Group (USA) Inc., 2010
Published by Speak, an imprint of Penguin Group (USA) Inc., 2011

1 3 5 7 9 10 8 6 4 2

THE LIBRARY OF CONGRESS HAS CATALOGED THE VIKING EDITION AS FOLLOWS:
Friend, Natasha, date—
For keeps / by Natasha Friend.
p. cm.
Summary: Just as sixteen-year-old Josie and her mother finally begin trusting men enough
to start dating seriously, the father Josie never knew comes back to town and shakes up
what was already becoming a difficult mother-daughter relationship.
ISBN 978-0-670-01190-2 (hardcover)
[1. Mothers and daughters—Fiction. 2. Dating (Social customs)—Fiction.
3. Single-parent families—Fiction. 4. Fathers and daughters—Fiction. 5. High schools—Fiction.
6. Schools—Fiction. 7. Family life—Massachusetts—Fiction. 8. Massachusetts—Fiction.]
I. Title.
PZ7.F91535For 2010
[Fic]—dc22
2009022472

Speak ISBN 978-0-14-241846-8

Set in Minion Regular.

Printed in the United States of America

For Emma Scarlett.

May you grow to be as kind as Kate,

as strong as Josie, and as bold as Liv.

One

IT'S THE LAST Friday night in August, and instead of dancing on a table at Melanie Jaffin's party with the rest of the soon-to-be junior class, I am crouched behind a tower of Meow Mix in the pet-food aisle of Shop-Co, watching my mother hyperventilate.

This is not new. Whenever we travel the fifteen miles from Elmherst, the town where we live, to North Haven, the town where my mom grew up—the only town with decent shopping—we risk running into someone she knew in high school, and we risk her wigging out. Right now she is sliding cat food around on a shelf so she can peer into the next aisle at whoever it is we're trying to avoid. Classic.

As I crouch, I make a mental list of everything I need for school: *three-ring binders, loose leaf, printer paper, pens . . .*

some of those highlighter markers. . . . I know I'm forgetting something, but I can't think of what.

My mother whirls around, bumping a bunch of Fancy Feast off a shelf. The cans careen down the aisle, like they're trying to get away from her.

"Mom?" I say. "Are you OK?"

She manages to look both crazy and adorable at the same time: blue eyes wide; tousles of blonde hair fluffing out every which way. It's the same hairstyle she's had since she was my age. She's always saying she needs to change it—grow it out, dye it red, something—but she never does.

"*Mom*," I say again, louder.

"Oh, God, Josie."

"What?" I say. Then, "Who is it?"

She shakes her head, like the name is too horrible to utter.

OK, now I have to look. Peering through the cat-food tunnel, I wonder who it will be. A bitchy former cheerleader? Or that math-geek guy we ran into at the recycling center a few months ago—the one in the Phish T-shirt and clogs—who made some lame joke about quadratic equations? He was cute, in a nerdy sort of way. When I pointed this out later, my mom told me about the time she barfed on his desk in trigonometry. I said, *That was a lifetime ago; he probably forgot.* And she said, *No one forgets the pregnant girl, Josie.*

Well, my mom doesn't have to worry tonight. Whoever

she is hiding from is gone. All I see is some tall, silver-haired couple, arguing about shampoo. He wants the Pert Plus; she says the store brand is a better value. He doesn't like the smell of the store brand; she says they smell exactly the same. Now she is unscrewing caps, holding up bottles, forcing him to sniff.

"The coast is clear," I tell my mom. "See? Just a couple of fogies fighting over hair products—and look, they're leaving. . . . *Now* can we get my stuff? You said this could be a quick stop, and I want to get to Mel's party before—"

"Josie," she says.

"Uh-huh." This whole time I've been trying to remember the other thing I need, and suddenly it comes to me. *Staples!* "Don't let me forget staples," I say, squatting to retrieve a can of Fancy Feast and return it to its shelf. "Binders, printer paper, pens—"

"Josie."

"Yeah."

"They're Paul's parents."

"What?" I grab another can, place it on the shelf.

"The couple with the shampoo. They're Paul Tucci's parents."

Paul Tucci.

The name zings through the air and impales me like an arrow. For a moment I can't breathe because . . . well, because sixteen-plus years ago Paul Tucci got my mother pregnant.

With me. He was a senior, she was a junior, and I was the size of a cocktail shrimp when his dad got transferred to a company in Arizona, and—even though Paul knew he had a kid in the making—he moved all the way across the country, and my mom never heard from him again.

It's the perfect Lifetime Television movie. Boy and Girl meet, fall in love, have sex; Girl gets pregnant; Boy falls off the face of the earth. Call me cynical, but from everything I know about Paul Tucci, it's hard to imagine a different ending.

I was in fifth grade the first time I asked my mom what happened. Up until then I had just accepted her vaguest of possible explanations: "You do have a father, Josie. He just lives in Arizona." But in fifth grade, I *really* asked. It was the night of the Spring Fling, this father-daughter dance at my school, and even though several of my friends' fathers had offered to bring me along too, I didn't want to get all dolled-up to drink punch and pretend to have fun fox-trotting with somebody else's dad. So I stayed home on the couch, eating popcorn with my mom. When I brought up the name Paul Tucci, she choked. Literally. She choked on a popcorn kernel, like the mere mention of his name caused her physical distress. But she tried to answer my questions. Questions like, *Why did he go AWOL? Does he have any shred of human decency? And, hello, isn't he even the least bit curious about how his kid turned out?*

Here is what she told me the night of the Spring Fling. Here are the facts, according to Kate Gardner:

Paul Tucci was a Big Deal in high school. Captain of the basketball team; top tenth percentile of his class; destined for greatness. (Kate Gardner was, in her own words, "destined for homecoming court and a job at the mall.") Paul Tucci's parents were Ivy League educated, as were his two older brothers. (Kate Gardner's parents hadn't gone to college.) The Tuccis had country club memberships. Seats on the town council. A ski condo in Waterville Valley *and* a beach house on the North Carolina coast. (The Gardners had none of these things—things that Kate's mother liked to refer to as "trappings of the rich and snooty.") The only thing Paul's parents and Kate's parents had in common, apparently, was their belief that no matter how in love Paul and Kate might be, they had no business dating each other.

But date they did. Against their parents' wishes. Behind their parents' backs.

To my fifth-grade self, of course, this sounded like the most romantic thing ever. Like *Romeo + Juliet*, the Leonardo DiCaprio version. I loved it that Paul Tucci and my mom were rebels. I loved it that when my mom found out she was pregnant, she and Paul decided not to tell anyone. They would keep the news to themselves for as long as they could—their little secret. But then, just like *Romeo and Juliet*, there was an unexpected plot twist: Paul's dad got transferred.

I hate unexpected plot twists.

I hate it that the Tuccis had to move to Arizona.

I hate it that—unlike Romeo—Paul Tucci turned out to be a spineless wanker who didn't have the guts to tell my mom about his new, not-so-pregnant, Arizona girlfriend. My mom had to find out the hard way, from Paul's best friend, Sully. On top of that, she had to tell her parents she was pregnant, drop out of high school junior year, and raise a baby.

Whenever I think about it, I get mad. Mad that Paul Tucci got off so easy. And, while I don't mean to imply that what happened was my mom's *fault* in *any* way—Paul Tucci is clearly a *negligent boob* that I don't even consider my father—I can't help but think that she could have tried a little harder to track him down and at least make him pay child support.

OK, I admit it. I am just the teeniest bit biased against Fathers Who Completely Shirk Their Parenting Responsibilities. Whenever I see one of those *Dateline* exposés about some deadbeat dad whose five kids are living in a trailer park eating moldy bread crusts while he's living it up in his high-rise apartment scarfing down filet mignon, it really gets to me. I mean, who do these guys think they are?

But in sixteen years, my mother has never asked Paul Tucci for anything. Not money, not even an explanation, and believe me there's a lot to explain. I have a thousand questions for him, if he ever decides to show up on our doorstep, begging to answer them. Needless to say he hasn't. Instead, on this random Friday night all these years later, his parents just materialize out of the ether. In the middle of Shop-Co.

No wonder my mom is hyperventilating.

Here we stand, the two of us, frozen in the pet-food aisle. And we don't even have a pet.

Carts roll by. Fluorescent lights buzz overhead. A voice announces a special on rotisserie chickens. *Only $5.99! Pick one up tonight!* Are Paul Tucci's parents on their way to the deli counter right now to pick up a hot, juicy rotisserie chicken? It's a real bargain. Why not get two? Why not buy the whole—

"I can't . . . believe they're here," my mother says. "How . . . are they here?" Her voice sounds high and squeaky, like a Muppet's. "Josie?" She is looking at me expectantly, as if I have the answers.

"I don't know," I tell her. "What I *do* know is we need to pick up these cans. OK? Can you help me with that?"

My best friend, Liv, likes to point out that whenever my mom starts acting like a kid, I start acting thirty-three. Liv says it's warped. I say it's the only way to survive in an emergency. Daughter gives instructions; mother follows. Grab a can; put it on a shelf. Grab a can; put it on a shelf.

When we're finished, she looks at me again.

"OK," I say. "We are going to get school supplies. After that, we are going to pay for them. And then you are going to drive me to Mel's party." I reach over to yank up the waist-band of her jeans so her underwear stops showing. "OK?"

She nods.

"And if we happen to see Paul Tucci's parents on the way, we are not going to freak, we are just going to keep walking, like we have no idea who they are. . . . Got it?"

She nods again.

"It's going to be OK," I add, because she seems to need the assurance.

The funny thing is, she's not like that. Ninety percent of the time, my mother is this amazingly smart, capable, beautiful, confident person. She doesn't cower behind cat food; she manages a bookstore. She reads *The New York Times*. She runs four miles every morning. My friends love her. A couple of them kind of worship her, actually. You do *not* want to play Scrabble with her, because she will kick your ass seven ways to Sunday with words you have never heard before. My mom is . . . well, she's just a great person, no matter what anyone who knew her in high school may think.

"See?" I say, as we're exiting the school-supplies aisle and rolling our cart toward the checkout. "Mission accomplished. That wasn't so bad, was it?"

By this point, my mother has relaxed into a yogalike calm. She's breathing normally. Her skin has regained its pinkish hue. *Crisis averted* is what I'm thinking.

Then, we see them again.

"Oh, God, Josie."

Paul Tucci's parents are in the checkout line, maybe thirty feet ahead of us.

"Oh, God. Shit."

She's regressing. And frankly, I don't think I'm up for Round Two. I don't want to spend another hour hiding out in, say, the feminine-hygiene aisle. I want to go to Melanie's party and dance on a table. Not literally. I'm not much of a table dancer. But the point is, I want to go and have fun with my friends. Because it's Friday night, and I'm sixteen years old, and I should be whooping it up, not holding my mother's hand while she has a breakdown.

"Shit, Josie. *Shit.*"

But here is the thing: She would do it for me. She *has* done it for me, a million times. She has rubbed my back while I've cried. She has held my hair while I've puked. When Marcus Weiner called me Turbo Tits in seventh grade, she took me out for ice cream and helped me craft a dozen witty comebacks. My mom has always been my greatest ally in times of crisis, even if she thought I was being a drama queen, even if she would rather have been doing something else at the time. And that is a beautiful thing. That is why, with all the daughterly love I can summon, I am now asking my mom to please remove her fingernails from my arm and hand me her wallet.

"What?" she says.

"Your wallet. Give it to me. I'll pay and meet you at the car."

"But . . . what if they . . ."

Her voice peters out, but I can tell what she was trying to say, and it almost makes me laugh. "It's not like they'll *recognize* me. They don't even know I *exist*."

As far as we know, this is true. As far as we know, Paul Tucci moved to Arizona without telling a single person what he left behind.

"Right." My mother smites her forehead. "Good point." And she hands me her wallet.

Of all the checkout lines, I had to plant myself behind Paul Tucci's parents. I just couldn't help myself. And now my heart is thumping against my tonsils.

Hi, I'm Josephine Gardner. You don't know me, but your son knocked up my mom.

No.

I'm Josie, your long-lost granddaughter.

No. These people aren't my grandparents, not really. The way I see it, I only have—had—one set of grandparents. My mom's parents, Homer and Eloise Gardner, whose house we now live in. They died when I was four, one after the other, from cancer. But I still remember little things. The way my grandfather smelled, like gin and butterscotch candies. And the wigs my grandmother wore—each one as dark and sleek as a panther pelt—to cover up her nearly hairless head. She kept them in a perfumed drawer in her closet. Sometimes she let me try them on.

Paul Tucci's mother's hair is metallic gray—a chin-length bob, parted on one side. Her shirt is crisp and white, but her khakis sag at the butt like a seventh-grade boy's. I would suggest a belt, but she'd probably slap my wrist the way she just slapped Paul's father's wrist when he tried to take a York Peppermint Pattie off the candy rack. "Put that back!" she told him. "No sweets!"

And he actually obeyed.

This shouldn't bother me—I don't even know these people—but still, who made her the queen? And come on, it's a Peppermint Pattie, not a crack pipe.

Maybe the issue is weight. Mr. Tucci is a big guy—not fat, exactly, but oxlike. Wide back, massive shoulders, huge tendony hands that can palm melons. Literally, this is what he's doing, palming two honeydews and holding them straight out in front of him like he's Michael Jordan. Or Frankenstein.

He's showing off a little, but Paul Tucci's mother doesn't seem to notice. She's too busy eyeballing the girl behind the counter—the one with the shaved head and the lip ring and the world's supply of black eyeliner. When the girl opens her mouth, you can see the stud in her tongue. "How're you folks doin' tonight?" she asks, friendly as can be.

Paul Tucci's mother gives her an icy "We're fine."

"Did you bring bags?"

"Shop-Co doesn't provide *bags*?"

"We do. We just try not to use them if we can help it."

"I beg your pardon?"

The girl juts her chin in my direction. "Reduce, reuse, recycle."

Now all eyes are on me—me and my canvas bags, which everyone I know carries. If you live within a fifty-mile radius of Elmherst, Massachusetts, you don't have a choice. *Keep Elmherst a Clean, Green Scene* isn't just a bumper sticker, it's a commandment.

But that's not really the point here. The point is, Paul Tucci's parents are looking at me, and I can feel my eyelid start to twitch—a little problem of mine whenever I get nervous.

Why am I nervous? To Paul Tucci's parents I am no one—just your average teenage girl in a Red Sox cap, virtually indistinguishable from any other teenage girl who might be buying school supplies tonight. So what if I have the same color eyes as them? A lot of people do. Brown eyes are a dominant trait. I learned that last year in bio, when we did a genetics unit.

Anyway, they've stopped looking at me. Mrs. Tucci is muttering under her breath to no one in particular that the whole world is turning into a hippie colony. It never used to be this way. Nobody used to care what kind of bags you used. *Blah, blah, blah.*

I would like to put a bag over her head.

Mr. Tucci doesn't say a word. He just pats her crisp white shoulder. *Pat-pat-pat.* As in, *There, there, honey. Everything's going to be OK.*

Is he used to her behavior, immune after so many years of marriage? I'm curious. Surely he knows she's being a jack-ass. Does he not mind?

It's an enigma to me, how two people can stay together. Despite their flaws, despite their most annoying habits. I don't get it, maybe because most of my friends' parents are divorced. Maybe because—with the exception of Paul Tucci—my mom has never dated anyone for more than a month. Maybe because the only "boyfriend" I've had was in eighth grade. Dan Applegate. We were together for thirteen days. He broke up with me in gym class—correction, his *friends* broke up with me in gym class. "Dan wants to see other people" is what they said, which was fine with me. I was perfectly content *not* getting felt up in the baseball dugout after school, preferring to lie on the couch in Liv's den watching *VH1 Behind the Music* and eating raw cookie dough.

So it's weird, seeing Paul Tucci's parents. Forget us being related, I mean the way they function as a couple. She orders; he obeys. She bitches; he pats. And somehow they manage to purchase three canvas bags, pack up their stuff, and stroll out of Shop-Co together, arm in arm.

*   *   *

"Josie! Where have you been?!"

Liv is standing on Melanie Jaffin's pool table.

"I've been waiting for you, like, forever!"

She is wearing a black feather boa, a red velvet smoking jacket, and a bikini.

"This place is insane! Did you see Michael Palamino?! No brain cells left! Seriously! Bumbling idiot! Get up here with me!"

Liv, stone-cold sober, starts Riverdancing to Eminem, and she couldn't care less what anyone in Mel's basement thinks. This is why I love her.

I have known Liv since we were six years old, when we first met on the swings at our neighborhood playground. She introduced herself as Olivia Sarah Weiss-Longo, told me she had two daddies, and said my hair looked like Snow White's. How could we not be best friends?

"I need to talk to you!" I'm screaming because it's the only way to be heard. The music is so, so loud.

Liv leaps off the pool table. *"Is everything OK? Are you— wait!"* She grabs my hand. *"Follow me!"*

As we wind our way through the bodies, I notice how good everyone looks tonight, tan and happy. Lots of people stop to hug us and scream things like, "OHMYGODYOU- GUYS! HOW WAS YOUR SUMMER?! CAN YOU BELIEVE WE'RE JUNIORS?!" Rob Vantine decides it's his mission in life to get us to drink the punch he made, with the orange slices floating on top, and the mango chunks stuck to the bottom. And, oh yeah, a gallon or two of vodka.

We graciously decline.

And press on.

Finally we make it to the upstairs bathroom, where every surface is coated with shaving cream. Yup; it's that kind of party. Melanie's father, who bought this lake house after he ditched Melanie's mother for his twenty-four-year-old paralegal, and who only gets to see Mel every third weekend, feels so guilty he lets her do whatever she wants.

"Huh," Liv says, looking around the bathroom. "Impressive." Then, being the fantastic friend that she is, she grabs a towel to mop the shaving cream off the side of the tub so we can sit. "So, what's up?"

"Well," I say, "there's been a Tucci sighting."

"*What?*"

"Yes."

"*WHAT?*"

"I know," I say. And tell her everything.

When I'm finished, my feather-boa-wearing, pool-table-hopping, Riverdancing best friend puts her hand on my arm. "Holy shite, Josie." (Liv prefers "shite" to "shit." She thinks it makes her sound British.)

"I know," I say.

"Do you think they moved *back*?"

"What?" I shake my head. "No. I'm sure they're just visiting old friends or something."

"How do you know?"

"What?"

"How do you know they're visiting old friends?"

"I don't know. They seemed . . . I mean, all they bought was shampoo and honeydews, and milk, and, like, toilet scrubbers—"

"*Toilet scrubbers?*"

"Yeah. So?"

Liv raises an eyebrow. "When was the last time you bought toilet scrubbers as a hostess gift?"

That's when it hits me. "Oh, God."

Liv says, "Exactly." Then she launches into one of her arguments, honed by many an afternoon of middle-school debate club. "Think about it, Jose. The *karma*. If his parents moved back, he has to show up sometime, right? For Thanksgiving or whatever? So unless you're planning to, like, never go to North Haven *again*, which would mean, basically, never buying anything *decent*, you are going to run into your dad. Which, come on, isn't that what you've always—"

"He's not my *dad*."

Liv nods. "OK."

"He will never be my dad."

"Right."

"He's just the guy who inadvertently gave me half my genetic material. He's . . . that's all he is."

"Yes," Liv says, bobbing her head. She used hot rollers tonight, and her curls are bobbing too.

I know she's humoring me. I know because the Paul Tucci argument is as old as our friendship. I know because the worst fight we've ever had was the time Liv e-mailed her hero, Dr. Steve, the world's most annoying TV therapist, suggesting a father-daughter reunion show. I saw the e-mail on her computer, and I went ballistic. She didn't do it to *hurt* me, she said at the time; she did it to *help* me. She threw out a lot of little gems like, *Listen, Josie, it's important to know the full story of where you came from. You may not like the choices your father made, but that doesn't mean he's not worth knowing. It doesn't mean you shouldn't forge some kind of relationship.*

Relationship? How about an acknowledgment of my *presence on Earth*? Let's start with *that*.

"OK, Josie," Liv says now. Her eyes are soft on mine. "Whatever you want to call him. I just think you should be, you know, mentally prepared to run into him."

She's probably right, but I don't want to talk about it. I don't even want to think about it.

Thankfully, this is the moment when Jamie Mann bursts through the bathroom door in her orange tie-dye tankini, both hands clapped over her mouth.

"Incoming," Liv murmurs, just as Jamie projectile vomits all over the floor, miraculously changing the subject.

Two

IT'S THE LAST day of preseason soccer. Coach is making us run until our feet fall off. School starts on Monday, and his torture sessions will shrink to two hours, so right now he's going psycho.

Sprint, reach down, touch a line, reverse. Sprint, reach down, touch a line, reverse.

"Gardner! You're slacking!"

I'm not slacking; I'm dying. Death by wind sprints.

Sprint, reach down, touch a line—

"Whaddja eat for breakfast, Gardner? Bowling balls? Come on! Get the lead out!"

Coach has this habit of sneaking up behind you and barking in your ear until you're going eighty. Usually it works.

Not today.

The problem is, I was up all night, and every cell in my body needs to be in bed. Bed, the one place I wanted to go after Mel's party but couldn't, because when I got home my mom was in the living room watching The Tapes. And that is never a good sign.

Whenever she gets stressed about something (e.g., seeing her long-lost ex-boyfriend's parents in Shop-Co), she busts out this box of ancient VHS tapes. Other people's parents might drink, or smoke, or inhale a box of Twinkies to feel better. My mother's drug of choice? *Beverly Hills, 90210*—the old-school version.

It's like some weird kind of therapy for her, watching angst-ridden teenagers act out their dramas. *Who will Kelly choose—Dylan or Brandon? Why is Brenda such a bitch? Will Donna* ever *have sex with David?* Even though my mom knows all the story lines by heart, she still watches the tapes over and over. She actually *cares* how things turn out for the characters, like they're her family, the siblings she never got to have. Which kind of makes me feel bad for her.

I felt especially bad last night, so even though I was tired after Mel's party, I sat next to my mom on the couch and watched *90210*, and ate the popcorn she made, and didn't mention the name Tucci once. No sense whacking her over the head with it. There would be plenty of time to discuss the possibility that Paul Tucci's parents have moved back.

A *possibility*. That's all it is.

But now, running sprints, a trickle of panic juice seeps into my head. What if they *did* move back? Will Paul Tucci show up? And if he does, will my mom be able to handle it? Will I?

I am still thinking about this when Coach blows his whistle, signaling the end of practice.

"Circle up, ladies!"

We run to the center of the field. It's me and Liv and Jamie Mann and Kara Ballensweig and Lindsey Ore, and all the other girls we've been playing with since fifth grade.

If we want to make it to states this year, Coach has to push us to get there, so even though we're gasping for air like beached fish right now, we kind of respect him for torturing us.

"On three," Coach says, and everyone puts their hands in the circle. "One, two, three—"

"TEAM!"

I remember when I first made varsity how I thought it was so cool to be shouting "Team!" instead of "Lady Hurricanes rock!" like we did in middle school. There I was, this skinny little freshman among seniors, shorts down to my ankles, bangs flopping in my eyes, feeling like I'd just won a spot at the Olympics. Now I'm one of the veterans. I'm also five foot nine—practically an Amazon—the second-tallest player on the team. If you saw me next to my mom you'd laugh. She's five three. Do I really need to mention where the height genes came from?

I try not to think about it, but sometimes, during a big game, when everyone else's father is in the stands, I imagine Paul Tucci showing up. I don't picture him waving to me or chanting my name or anything, just being there. I know it sounds stupid. And anyway, who needs a father when you've got a mother like Kate Gardner, the human megaphone? *(Go, Josie! Goooooo, Josie! Shoot! Shooooot!)*. Or when you've got Liv's two dads—Pops and Dodd—sitting next to my mom, banging cowbells like mad?

Liv and I laugh about it now, but when we were in second grade—before we knew any better—we tried to convince my mom to marry Pops or Dodd so we could be a "real" family. We had the whole wedding planned. We would be the flower girls, of course; Liv's brother, Wyatt, would be the ring bearer; and the cake would be three-tiered, white with pink roses. Whichever dad didn't get to marry my mom would be the DJ and play the *Grease* soundtrack.

Somehow no one else seemed to think this was a great idea, so Liv and I eventually gave up the dream of being related and settled for our parents being friends. Which they still are. They do things like cook dinner for each other on the weekends and bring in each other's newspapers when it's raining and drive each other's kids around after practice.

"Need a ride home?" Liv asks as we walk from the field to the locker room. She's wearing the vintage '70s soccer jersey she found in the bargain bin at Retro Ruby's, with the green and yellow collar flapping out to her shoulders so it looks like she has wings. Her hair is braided and pinned up in two Princess Leia buns. Only Liv could pull this off.

"Not home," I tell her. "Work."

"Since when do you work Saturdays?"

"Since Bob changed the schedule."

"*Again?*"

"Yup."

Last year, when I first started working at Bananarama, I thought I'd landed the easiest job on the planet. I mean, how hard could it be to scoop ice cream? But that was before I realized Boss Bob's obsessive-compulsive tendencies. Not only does he switch the schedule around every ten minutes, he also insists that the spoons be lined up in perfectly symmetrical rows on the counter and that every sprinkle be picked up off the floor before we close at night. Bob will have a hissy if I'm late for work, but right now I'm too thirsty to care.

Liv and I stand in line at the water fountain to fill our bottles. When we're finished, we start to enter the locker room, but something grabs our attention. It's the boys' team. Two dozen pairs of legs, sweaty and dirt streaked. Two dozen sets of cleats, clacking against the pavement.

Look at us, the guys command. *Ogle away. You know you're powerless not to. That's right, keep looking.*

And really, it's hard to do anything else. Especially for certain members of our team—the ones who would rather talk about boys than play soccer. The Makeup Mafia, Liv and I secretly call them, because they actually care what they look like on the field.

Right now Lindsey and Jamie and this other girl Schuyler are flipping their hair all around and sticking out their boobs because the guys are approaching. It's kind of fascinating to watch, the way they fluff themselves up like peacocks whenever a little testosterone appears.

Then there's me, with the pit-sweat circles down to my waist, and the hair sliding out of its ponytail and sticking to my cheeks. And the gummy white stuff that I know for a fact is stuck in the corners of my mouth, but I refuse, on principle, to wipe away.

So what if Matt Rigby is looking at me right now? So what if he's a senior and his body looks like it was chiseled from pure marble like Michelangelo's *David*?

If Riggs is going to stare at me with those big blue eyes, I am going to stare back, but if he thinks I'm about to wipe the schmutz off my face just to impress him, he can forget it.

"Hey," he says, holding my gaze.

"Heyyy, Riggsy," Lindsey and Jamie and Schuyler chorus together. Their voices sound five octaves higher than normal.

I say nothing. I just continue the staring contest that's been going on for the past seven months.

We have this history, Matt Rigby and I. Last year, when I was a sophomore and he was a junior, there was this New

Year's Eve party and I needed a ride home, so he drove me. Riggs had a girlfriend at the time, Missy Travers, a senior who was also my soccer captain. Not only was Missy beautiful, she was a great captain. Before every game, she would type up these little slips of paper with inspirational quotes on them, and we would stick the slips of paper in our shin guards. She would give us rubber bands to put on our wrists, and whenever we screwed up we'd have to snap the rubber bands to make ourselves forget our mistake, because if we dwelled on it then our game would be messed up.

Everyone loved Missy. And because Missy and Riggs had been an established couple for more than a year, I didn't give it a thought when he offered to drive me home from the party. Missy was in Quebec for a week, on the Canadian-U.S. exchange. It wasn't like Riggs had anything better to do that night. He was just being a nice guy, I thought, walking me from his car to my front door. The sidewalk was icy. He didn't want me to slip.

It was also crazy cold, I remember, and I wasn't exactly dressed for the weather. I had on the green silk shirt I'd borrowed from my mother, black leggings, and ballet flats. If I'd been wearing heels I would have been taller than Riggs, but because of the flats we were the same height. So when he smiled at me under the porch light, his mouth was right across from mine.

I don't know how it happened, exactly. One minute we

were talking and the next he was leaning in, pressing his lips to my neck. At the same time, his fingers were tracing the outline of my body—shoulders to ribs to waist to hips to the tops of my thighs—so softly I shivered. He must have thought I was cold because he wrapped his arms around my back and kissed me again, this time on the lips.

Matt Rigby is kissing me! That's what I was thinking. Followed by, *He is such a good kisser. How did he get to be such a good kisser?* Followed by, *Oh, God.*

That's when I pulled away, which was not the easiest thing to do. (His lips tasted like cherry ChapStick, which I happen to love.)

"What's wrong?" Riggs said, innocent as can be.

And I said, "What about Missy?"

He looked me straight in the eye and said that he and Missy had "an agreement." While she was away, the two of them could do whatever they wanted, with whoever they wanted to do it. If Missy wanted to kiss some guy named Pascal, for instance, on the ice at some Canadian hockey rink, that was A-OK.

I didn't think Missy would do that—I knew for a fact that she kept an eight-by-ten picture of Riggs in her locker, and she actually kissed it before practice—but I let myself believe what he told me. I let myself do all sorts of things that night. . . . Clothing was removed. . . . Certain body parts were touched. . . .

Now whenever Riggs looks at me, I feel a little zing down my spine, a combination of hormones and guilt. Not that Missy ever found out what happened between us. I would have heard if she had; the Elmherst High School grapevine works fast. All I know is when she came home from Quebec, it was business as usual for the two of them—holding hands in the caf, cheering at each other's games, prom. She probably never even noticed the way Riggs would look at me whenever our paths crossed, which is the same way he is looking at me right now. His *come-hither look*, Liv calls it.

Liv thinks the whole thing is hilarious. When Riggs and I finally break eye contact and enter our separate locker rooms, she elbows me in the ribs. "Easy, Hester," she says. As in Hester Prynne. As in *The Scarlett Letter*, which we read in sophomore lit and which has haunted me ever since.

"Ha-ha," I say.

Liv thinks now that Missy and Riggs have broken up and Missy has left for Stanford, I should stop feeling so bad about what happened last year and "jump his bones already." Liv says the sexual tension is so thick between us, "you could chop it with a hatchet." She is full of little nuggets of sex wisdom that she gets from the magazines Dodd brings home from the hair salon where he works. Liv's message is always the same: *Look, Josie, you can't stay a virgin forever, and you certainly don't want to be one of those poor girls who hold out until college and lose it on a La-Z-Boy at a frat party, so what are you waiting for?*

Well, I'll tell you what I'm waiting for. I'm waiting for a guy who's not going to break my heart. Is that so crazy?

Not that I've experienced heartbreak firsthand, but I look at my mom and her deer-in-the-headlights approach to dating, and I get it. She's been crushed. She doesn't want to start all over with some new guy, just to get blindsided by another Arizona girlfriend.

I hate that Paul Tucci broke my mother's heart, but to be honest, a small, secret part of me is glad he did. If he hadn't, I wouldn't know what I know, which is that a girl has to protect herself. And I don't mean Trojans! Because no matter what those sex-ed teachers say about how great condoms are, there's not a condom in the world that can protect you from heartbreak.

When I get to work, Boss Bob is on his knees, scrubbing the floor with his bare hands. This is supposed to be my job, *after* the customers leave, and I use a mop. But sometimes Bob can't help himself. He also can't help disinfecting the ice-cream scoopers and wiping nonexistent caramel smears off the counter every two seconds. Scrub, scrub, scrub. Wipe, wipe, wipe. It's like his mission in life, to make everything sanitary. I almost feel bad for him, but then I think, *If you hate messes so much, why run an ice-cream shop? Why not a bleach factory?*

The fact is, Bob does hate Bananarama. The only reason he works there is he inherited the business from his parents.

Ever since they died, he's been coming up with new business schemes. First he wanted to start a bead shop. After that it was a pizza parlor. For the past few months his big dream has been to open Elmherst's first European-style café. FedEx packages keep arriving on the doorstep. Not that Bob tells me what's in them. My job isn't to ask questions; it's to lug boxes down to the basement and stack them in perfectly symmetrical rows against the back wall. Bob is *just a bit* of a control freak.

"You're late," he says now, looking up from the floor. His eyebrows imply half an hour, not five minutes.

"I know," I say. "I'm sorry."

I slip on my brown polyester apron with its smattering of embossed sprinkles. *Bananarama! Forty-one Flavors of Fun!*

"I need you to restock the napkin dispensers," Bob says. At full height, his head comes up to my shoulder. His hair is a coppery fringe around a shiny circle of scalp—quite possibly the cleanest scalp in the universe.

"No problem," I tell him.

"Did you wash your hands?"

Of course I washed my hands. Hand washing is Commandment Number One around here, like this is the ER, and every day we're performing surgery on the pope.

Bottom line: I need to wash again.

I walk to the sink and turn on the hot water.

"Mom working today?" Bob asks. As if he doesn't know.

Twilight Books is two stores down from Bananarama, and my mom's Volkswagen—aka the Green Hornet—is parked outside.

Bob's crush on my mother is so obvious, it's painful to behold. *Give it up*, I want to tell him. *It's never going to happen.* Instead I nod and say, "Yeah. She's working today."

Of course, I can't blame Bob for feeling the way he feels. He isn't the first, and he certainly won't be the last to fall under the Kate Gardner spell. In eighth grade, my earth science teacher, Mr. Bond, could barely get the words out around her at Parents' Night. He kept saying the same thing: "Y-You're . . . J-Josie's mother?" Then there was the cable guy, Russell, who after he installed our modem made about five hundred excuses to drop by and see how things were "working out." There's Len from the post office. And Kara Ballensweig's dad, who flirts with my mom during soccer games, even with Kara's mother sitting right there. I could go on and on. But now, as I'm beginning to fill the napkin dispenser, Bob is snapping his fingers in my face.

"You have a customer." *Snap, snap.* His hands are milky white and pudgy at the knuckles, like a toddler's. "Customers *first*. Napkins *after*. OK?"

"OK," I say. Bob is such a stress ball. It can't be healthy. I want to tell him to close his eyes and breathe, picture a babbling brook. Instead, I assume the ice-cream position. "Welcome to Bananarama! Forty-one Flavors of Fun!"

I know. The first time I said those words I felt like a moron. But I'm used to it now.

"What do you think, monkeys?" It's a woman with frizzy red hair, about my mom's age, and two freckly boys in matching dump-truck shirts. "Pistachio? Butter pecan? Peach?"

They take about a year to decide, which doesn't surprise me. Forty-one is too many choices for a kid.

Finally, the mother orders—two chocolate cones, waffle variety, with sprinkles, rainbow for Joel and, uh—"Do you want sprinkles, Matt? . . . Chocolate or rainbow? . . . OK, Matt wants rainbow too."

Matt.

Well, now my cheeks are burning and I'm glad to have an excuse to stick my head in the freezer.

I am *so* not going to think about Matt Rigby right now. In fact, I'm not going to think about him for the rest of the day. Because, let me tell you, I have many more worthwhile things to think about.

Three

LIV'S DADS INVITE us for Sunday dinner. It's a two-part celebration: me, Liv, and Wyatt going back to school and Dodd's promotion at work. Now instead of being Trillium Salon and Day Spa's assistant stylist, he's the expert colorist. This may not sound like a big deal, but Pops couldn't be prouder. There's shrimp on the grill, champagne, and a huge cake in the shape of a woman's head, with yellow Twizzlers for hair.

Liv made up business cards on her computer: *Todd Longo, Colorist to the Stars.* Todd is his real name. When Liv was little she couldn't pronounce her T's, and "Dodd" just stuck.

Now, about fifteen minutes into dinner, Pops starts telling the story of how he and Dodd met.

"So he took one look at me and said, 'Sweet Christ, what are we going to *do* with all that *hair?*'"

Even though she's heard the story a million times, my mom throws back her head and laughs. I do too. Because the thing is, Pops does have crazy hair—thick and dark and curly. When it grows out, it becomes a Jackson Five fro, which is pretty funny when you think about where he works: Sterling, Weiss & Lowe, this ultraconservative law firm in Worcester. Pops is Gregory James Weiss—the "Weiss" in Sterling, Weiss & Lowe. He wears custom-made suits to work every day.

Dodd wears jeans.

Pops is also a sports fanatic, whereas Dodd couldn't hit a baseball if his life depended on it. Pops drinks scotch; Dodd drinks Fresca. Basically, if you didn't know how perfect they were together, you'd take one look at them and think, *Huh?* But Pops and Dodd are, bar none, the happiest couple I know.

Which makes it all the more cringe-worthy when halfway through the meal Pops turns to my mom and says, "So, Kate. I heard you had quite the shopping trip the other night."

Come on. Does Liv really need to tell her dads everything? Is nothing sacred?

My mom gives me a look. I kick Liv under the table.

"Ow!"

Liv's twelve-year-old brother, Wyatt, raises his eyebrows at me. "Kidney stone?"

"*What?*"

"You seem to be in pain. When Pops had one, he said it hurt like—"

"Oh, honey," Dodd says, reaching out to caress my mom's hand. "How *are* you?" His green eyes are wide with tragedy, as if instead of seeing Paul Tucci's parents buying shampoo, my mom had witnessed a murder.

"I'm fine," she says, waving a shrimp through the air. "Absolutely fine. . . . I haven't even thought about it."

Bald-faced lie. I saw the yearbook on her bed last night, and I know she was looking at Paul Tucci's picture. Maybe the close-up—his senior portrait. Or the full-body shot of him at the foul line, shooting a free throw. If that's not "thinking about it," what is?

"Thought about *what*?" Wyatt says. His long strawberry-blond bangs flop gracefully over one eye—the latest of Dodd's creations.

"Kate ran into some old friends at the grocery store," Pops explains. "Some friends she hadn't expected to see again."

And the Euphemism of the Year Award goes to . . .

"Josie's dad's parents," Liv says, which compels me to kick her under the table once more. And once more she says, "Ow!" Then, "What?" Liv looks from me to my mom and back to me. "We all know the story. What's the big secret? We're family!"

My mom nods and jams the fork in her mouth. She chews for a second, then blurts out something that sounds like "Family comes in many forms," sending little bits of shrimp sailing through the air like confetti.

Wyatt cocks an eyebrow at her. "Say it, don't spray it."

And my mom laughs. If anyone is a good sport, it's Kate Gardner. If anyone is going to smile and say, "Now, how 'bout that hair cake?" it's my mom.

Still, I know she's hurting. Those Tuccis are stuck in her brain like shards of glass. But she's not going to let on, believe me.

I watch as my mom raises her glass to Dodd. "To the best expert colorist this side of the Mississippi."

"Hear, hear!" Pops says.

"Hair, hair!" my mom says, and everyone laughs.

I love this about her, the way she makes other people feel like a million bucks. Instead of throwing a pity party for herself, she's always the first to say "Good for you" to someone else. It's a wonderful trait. Also kind of twisted. I mean, why should Kate Gardner, this amazingly caring and giving person, not have what Pops and Dodd have? Someone who loves her back? Even someone who is completely tone-deaf like Pops, who right now is holding up the hair cake and singing, *"Isn't she loooovely"* at the top of his lungs while Dodd gazes up at him with big, starry eyes. It's the sweetest thing ever. Sweeter than hair cake.

It's 7:40 a.m. and I am back on Liv's porch, ringing the doorbell. Since Liv is a May birthday and I'm June, all we have is our learner's permits. We can't drive to school yet, so we figured we'd ride the bus like we have every day since first grade (Liv: window seat, me: aisle), but for some reason my mom insisted on chauffeuring. Now she is sneaking little glances at us in the rearview mirror and saying things like, "Junior year. I can't believe it. This is huge."

She's fresh from the shower, fully caffeinated, and smiling, but I can just see the thought bubble rising over her head: *Junior year. The year my life went to hell in a handbasket.* My mom only got to be a junior for three months. Three months before she peed on a stick and saw that little pink plus sign.

"One more year and you'll be seniors," she says. "*Two* more and you'll be in college."

College, the one place my mother never got to go. Instead she got her GED. And a big, fat belly.

One time I asked her why she didn't go back to high school after I was born, to finish her senior year, and she said, "It wasn't my choice, Josie." It was Grandma Gardner who wanted her to work, who pushed her to take the job at the bookstore.

"*College,*" my mom says again, shaking her head. "I can't believe it."

"I know, right?" Liv says, shaking her head right along with my mom. "*Six* more years and we won't even *be* in school."

You would think that Liv, being an expert in the art of sarcasm delivery, is mocking my mother, but she's not. Liv loves school. There is no one, and I mean *no one* who embraces the first day like Olivia Weiss-Longo. For as long as I can remember, she has been the kid with the fifty-pack of perfectly sharpened #2 pencils in her book bag and an apple for the teacher.

She's also the one in the crazy outfit. In middle school, if all the girls were wearing jeans on the first day, Liv would show up in a peasant dress. If miniskirts were the rage, she'd wear camouflage. Liv is so anti-cool, she actually raises coolness to new heights. So I had to laugh when I saw her this morning, in kneesocks and a plaid kilt fastened with one of those giant safety pins. I guarantee tomorrow half the freshman girls will be wearing the same thing.

At a stoplight, Liv scrambles into the front seat next to my mom. "O licensed driver over the age of twenty-one, can I drive?"

"No, you may not."

"Why not?"

"Because if I let you drive, then I would not have the pleasure of chauffeuring you on the first day of your junior year."

"Pleeeeeease, Kate?"

"Noooooooo, Liv."

Liv pretends to pout, but she doesn't mean it. She loves my mom. My mom is the mom Liv never got to have. Her and Wyatt's biological mother is an egg donor/surrogate from Minnesota, a Princeton grad with a genius IQ. Pops and Dodd joke about this, saying next year Liv can apply to Princeton as a legacy, but we all know she's so smart she would get in anyway.

"Who do you have for English?" I ask from the backseat.

Liv looks at her schedule. "Uh . . . Montrose. Fifth period."

"AP?"

"Yup."

Advanced Placement English. I rest my case. I'm about to ask about math when Liv changes the subject. "Look, Jose," she says, pointing out the window. "Wendy Geruntino is wearing a thong!"

Sucker that I am, I look.

Wendy Geruntino, walking along the sidewalk with the same wheely pink backpack she's had since seventh grade, is wearing baggy jeans and a sweater down to her knees.

"Ha-ha," I say.

Liv crosses her eyes and grins.

Wendy Geruntino would never in her life wear a thong. Wendy Geruntino is secretary of the student council and co-chair of the Christian Students Fellowship. She is also the founder and president of Elmherst High School's Chastity Club, which is essentially a society for virgins. Last year in assembly she tried to get the entire student body to sign a purity pledge, inspiring a bunch of senior guys to yell, "Eat me!" from the back of the auditorium.

It's mind-boggling how Wendy keeps up the cause, trying to convince everyone to "stay pure" until marriage, when ninety percent of the school rags on her.

"I don't know why anyone would wear a thong," my mom says. "They seem so uncomfortable."

"Don't knock it till you try it, Kate," Liv says.

"Please," I say. "Don't encourage her."

The last thing I need is my mom showing up to one of my soccer games in dental-floss underwear. It's bad enough that she's barely aged since high school—that her butt looks as good in low-rise jeans as my friends' do, and that guys my own age check her out. She's my *mother*.

We pull up to the curb in front of school.

"Junior year," my mom says again, gripping the steering wheel. "I still can't believe it." She leans over to kiss Liv's cheek, then turns back to me.

"J-Bear."

There's no stopping her from using that nickname or from flinging her arms around my neck, burying her nose in my ear, and whispering how proud she is of me.

Minutes pass, and she's not letting go.

"Mom," I say.

Liv has hopped out of the car and our friends are beginning to gather on the sidewalk, whispering, laughing.

"*Mom*. Everyone's waiting."

Finally—and I can tell how hard this is for her to do—she tears herself away.

A lot of my friends would be rolling their eyes by now, saying, *God, Mother. There's a reason teenagers don't let their parents drive them to school.*

But I don't say that. Instead I say, "It's just another school year."

My mom nods, smiles a little. "I know." She eyes the shirt I'm wearing, gauzy and white, with the lace camisole underneath—tight, but not too tight. "Are you sure you don't want a sweater? I have a sweater in the—"

"Mom," I say.

"OK, OK." She holds up her hands.

"Just . . . I'll be fine."

"I know."

"OK?"

She nods.

"I'll stop by the store tonight."

"Sounds good."

"Good," I say, and hop out of the car to join my friends.

My mother beeps, waves, drives away.

And what do I feel? Relief. OK, and a tiny sprinkling of guilt on top. But that is not going to stop me, let me tell you. This is my junior year! *My* junior year, and I have no intention of screwing it up.

I sit in the back row of Mr. Catenzaro's homeroom, between Kimmy Gustofson and Lorelei Hill, who screamed when they saw me and launched right in, telling me every detail of their summers. They were both lifeguards at Lake Wyola (big shocker there; Kimmy and Lorelei have been attached at the hip since kindergarten). They both dated fellow lifeguards (uh-uh). Total hotties (of course). Who just so happened to be twin brothers: Andy and Randy (ach).

Fluorescent lights crackle overhead. The air is a potpourri of chalk dust, armpits, and those wood shavings the janitor throws on the floor when someone pukes.

I notice that Mr. Catenzaro, who is the only teacher I know who wears jeans to school, seems to have gone one denim shade darker and two sizes tighter since last year. Liv thinks Mr. C is hot. She says he looks just like John Travolta in *Saturday Night Fever*—the same olive skin; dark, feathered hair; chin dimple. She imagines him tossing off his blazer after school, unbuttoning his shirt, and doing the hustle on his desk. I'm not sure how she comes up with these things, but she does.

It's not just Mr. C, either. Liv thinks a lot of the male teachers are hot. Even Mr. Arble, the assistant principal, with his cheesy goatee, makes it onto her crush list. *Forget high-school boys*, Liv is always telling me. Too immature. The last guy she dated, Avi, a counselor at her drama camp, was twenty-one: a real man.

The truth is, twenty-one sounds old to me—skeevy. I like *boys*. I like that Matt Rigby was a bit unsure of himself that night on my porch, fumbling with the hook on my bra, embarrassed when our noses bumped. If he was twenty-one instead of seventeen, he might not have been so—

"Josephine? . . . Josephine Gardner?"

Mr. Catenzaro must have been calling my name for a while, because now everyone is looking at me. I can feel my cheeks heat up.

"Here," I say.

Mr. C grins. "Are you sure about that?" His teeth are big and square and white. "Sure you're not still on the beach somewhere?"

Porch swing, actually.

I bob my head like an idiot, telling myself: *No—the whole class did* not *just watch a slow-motion reenactment of Matt Rigby de-bra-ing you on New Year's Eve.*

Mr. C finishes attendance and moves on to announcements. My cheeks return to room temperature. After a million years, the bell rings.

By some scheduling fluke, the entire Makeup Mafia ends up in fourth-period gym with me and Liv.

"So *their* coach talked to Coach, and I think it's happening tomorrow." Jamie Mann is all smiles and hair flips.

I sit on the bleachers, lacing up my sneakers and listening to Jamie, Kara, Lindsey, and Schuyler chattering away.

"It is *such* an awesome idea," Kara says.

"I know, right?" Lindsey says.

"Isn't it an awesome idea?"

"Don't you guys think?"

Apparently, they're asking me and Liv.

"About what?" Liv says.

"Coed scrimmage. With the boys' team." Jamie's face is all aglow with excitement.

"Whose idea was it?" I ask.

"Theirs," Schuyler says. "Can you believe it?"

No, actually. I can't.

"Their strength is aggression at the net," Jamie explains. "And we're better at the passing game, so it, like, makes sense to learn from each other."

"Plus if we're trying to impress each other, we'll probably play better. I know *I* will," Schuyler says. Schuyler is not exactly the queen of motivation during practice. She's probably most excited about scrimmaging the guys so she can show off her butt in Spandex.

Liv shrugs. "Sounds good to me." Meanwhile, her elbow is digging into my ribs. "Hester?"

I shoot Liv the fish-eye.

She smiles innocently.

The girls are confused. "Who's Hester?"

"No one," I say. "Scrimmage sounds fun."

Seventh period, on my way to English, I'm walking through the senior corridor (not because I'm hoping to run into anyone, but because it's the shortest route to Room 310), and I see him. Matt Rigby, alone at his locker, fiddling with the padlock. His polo shirt is bright green, new-looking. Blond hair curls over his collar. Jeans. Black Converse low tops. I can feel my breath quicken, the plunge of my stomach into my knees. He couldn't look better if he tried.

What if I walked up to him right now? What if I walked right up and tapped him on the shoulder—smiled and tossed my hair around like Jamie Mann. *Hey, Riggsy. What's up?*

But I would never do that.

It's stupid to pretend that I don't see him, but that's what I do. I hold my books to my chest and steer my gaze to the end of the hall: the trophy case under the Elmherst Hurricanes banner.

Out of the corner of my eye I see a redhead in a tube top—Tessa something, a senior—sidle up next to him. "Heyyy, Riggsy!" she says in that perky cheerleader way, draping one arm around his waist like she's done it a million times before.

She wants to know if he's going to study hall. He is? Great! They can go together!

Great.

"Are you going to the game Friday night?" I hear her ask.

And he says, "I don't know. I have to check with my secretary." Now she giggles.

I walk as fast as a person can walk without looking like a moron.

Sometimes the feeling is like a wrecking ball to your gut. Not that I have any right to be jealous. I mean, just because Matt Rigby disrobed me on a porch swing once, it's not like I own the guy. He's probably been disrobing girls all summer long, ever since he and Missy broke up. And who cares if he has? Matt Rigby can do whatever he wants, as far as I'm concerned. It's a free country.

"Awww," my mom says. "Best daughter in the world." She peels back the lid of the milk shake I've brought her and tastes it. "Hmm. White chocolate peanut butter?" She likes to be surprised, so Bob always changes it for her. "No, wait"—she frowns into the cup—"what is that? Almond? Cashew?"

"Macadamia nut," I say. "White chocolate macadamia nut."

"Aha!"

"Bob says hi, by the way."

"Well, tell him hi back."

"If I do that, he'll think you like him."

She smiles. "Bob's sweet."

"Please." I roll my eyes. "I have ten minutes before I have to go back and bleach something."

"And I have no customers. Let's sit." She steps down from the ladder she's been using to shelve books. We're in the travel section. I used to love the travel section. When I was little I would pull down the National Geographic coffee-table books with the photos of Africa, and I'd pretend I was going on safari. Now I'm more into self-help. That section is hilarious. Whatever problem you're having, there's a book with the solution. Fear of snakes? Check out the *Phobia and Anxiety Workbook*. Trouble with your hoo-hoo? You too can *Overcome Painful Vaginal Symptoms and Enjoy an Active Lifestyle*. Then there's my personal favorite—the first place everyone should turn when they're feeling sorry for themselves: *Shut Up, Stop Whining, and Get a Life*.

We plop onto the blue velvet couch by the window. Everything in Twilight Books comes in shades of blue. Blue curtains, blue chairs, blue shag rugs. This color scheme can be either extremely soothing or extremely depressing, depending on your mood.

"So," my mom says, "how was the first day?"

I shrug. "OK."

"OK?" Both eyebrows shoot up.

Here is the thing: You can't just say "OK" to my mother. You can't just say "fine." You have to get specific. There is no such thing as the fuzzy middle.

"Teacher stuff, girl stuff, or boy stuff?" she asks.

I shake my head.

"It's one of the three."

"How do you know?"

"I know."

"How?"

She laughs. "Believe it or not, I used to be a sixteen-year-old girl."

"Gee, really?" I say, adding a little squirt of sarcasm. "I had no idea."

She takes a sip of milk shake. Stirs it with her finger. Licks the finger. Takes another sip. Waits.

"If you must know," I say, "it's boy stuff."

"*The* boy?"

I nod. My mom knows about New Year's Eve—the PG version anyway.

She leans in.

I sigh, reach for the milk shake, take a swallow. "This is disgusting."

"You're changing the subject," she says.

"No, I'm not."

"So . . . did you talk yet?"

"I told you, we don't *talk*. We stare. And we say nothing. That's what we do."

My mom raises her eyebrows again.

"Just . . . never mind. It's not a big deal."

Silence for a moment. Then she pats my arm. "Well, you'll talk to him when you're ready."

"What's that supposed to mean?"

"When you're ready to put yourself out there, to take the risk, you'll do it."

"Oh, OK, Pot."

"What?"

"Calling the kettle black much? When was the last time you put yourself out there?"

"We weren't talking about me," she says.

I smile. "We are now."

She gives me a look that's halfway between annoyed and amused. *Anused? Ammoyed?*

"When was the last time you went on a date? Huh? 1994?"

I am referencing the Paul Tucci era without actually saying the name. I can't. My mother hasn't uttered the word "Tucci" since the Shop-Co debacle, which means she is not exactly—

"Help!" I squeal, because she is pinching my thigh. "Child abuse!"

That's when the bells above the front door tinkle and a man walks in. Not too old, not too young. Blue eyes, wavy sand-colored hair. Suede jacket, khakis. Funky green sneakers. He spots us on the couch. "Wait—you *are* open, right?"

"Absolutely," I say, and stand up.

"Great," the guy says. Nice baritone voice. "Because I'm looking for a book."

"Break's over," I say to my mom, and boy do I hightail it out of there. Because sometimes, just when you need to end a conversation, a beautiful moment arrives.

Four

THE NEXT MORNING my mom makes pancakes, which is not normal. Most of the time it's toast or cereal. I sit at the kitchen counter, watching her slide pancakes onto a platter like Martha Stewart.

"What's his name again?" I ask.

"Jonathan."

"Jonathan," I repeat. "Not Jon?"

"I don't think so," my mom says, shaking her head. "No." She opens her mouth, closes it.

"What?" I say.

"Nothing."

I can tell she wants to say more, but she doesn't want to jinx it. She's probably saying to herself: *Come on, Kate. He's just a guy who came into the store looking for a book.* (Except that the book just happened to be *The World Is Flat*, which my mom just happened to have finished reading last week, and which just happened to jump-start a two-hour conversation.)

"He'll be back," I say.

"You think?" She pours juice into my cup, which already has juice.

"Yes."

She sits down next to me but doesn't say anything for a minute. "It's just . . ."

"What?"

"It's been a long time since I . . ."

"*What?*" I say, even though I know. Two words, rhymes with "Saul Crucci." It's been a long time since she felt anything even remotely close to the way she felt in high school.

"I don't know!" she says. "Just . . . I know it sounds crazy. We just met! But there was something there last night."

"What kind of something?"

"Something . . . I don't know. . . . I'm being ridiculous."

"No, you're not," I say.

She shakes her head.

"You're *not*, Mom."

She shrugs, smiles.

"I get it," I say. Because I do. I get that she's giddy and insecure and scared and hopeful and utterly confused. All because of a guy.

"I guess I'll go for a run," she says.

"Do it," I say.

"You'll take the bus?"

"Unless you want to give me the car. I'm an excellent driver. . . ."

"I will give you the car when you get your license."

"Fine," I mock-grumble. "Be that way."

But then I hug her and say thanks for the pancakes. "I could get used to this," I tell her. "What do I get when he asks you out? Eggs Benedict?"

My mom snorts. I snort back. She snorts again, louder. This is how the Gardner Girls do the levity thing: We impersonate livestock.

"Close your eyes," Liv says on the bus.

"What?"

"Just do it. I have something for you."

"Fine." I close my eyes. "I don't know why you have to be such a—"

"Open!"

She's holding up a piece of paper. It's a photo of a house— a humongo white colonial with a three-car garage and a circular driveway.

"So?"

Liv smiles. "So . . . Nico and Christina Tucci. Forty-four Lehigh Street. North Haven, Massachusetts."

"*What?*"

"I know, right? They closed two weeks ago."

"But how did you—?"

"One of Dodd's clients at Trillium runs a real-estate agency. . . . Anyway, it's a matter of public record."

All I can do is stare at her.

"I thought you should have the information," she says. "You know . . . just in case."

"In case *what*?"

Liv shrugs. "In case you decide to get in touch."

"I *won't*."

"Well . . ."

"Like, *ever*."

"Completely your call." She folds the paper in half, then in quarters. "We'll just put this away for now." She unzips the side pocket of my backpack, slides the paper in. "For safe-keeping."

"You're unbelievable. Do you know that?"

"So I've been told."

All day in school I've been thinking about the Tuccis. But I'm not going to think about them anymore. I am done. *Finito.* The only thing I'm going to think about right now is the fact that it rained last night and the fields are soaked for our coed scrimmage.

The coaches spend ten minutes bitching about the lack of

drainage and another ten debating the merits of playing in a swamp versus preserving the grass. Finally they decide we should just use the baseball field because their season doesn't start until spring, and their grass will grow back by then.

They split us into teams by position until we're evenly matched. I'm on the blue team. So is Liv. Matt Rigby is on the gold team, and try as I might not to notice these things, I do: The gold pinny matches his hair.

How pathetic am I?

So pathetic.

I am not, however, pathetic enough to be wearing either "Juicy"-across-the-butt shorts (Schuyler) or blue eye shadow (Jamie) in honor of the occasion. No. I am my usual slobby soccer-playing self, because I didn't come to this scrimmage to impress anyone. I came here to play soccer.

It's a mudfest. There's no other way to describe it. Here's what happened: About fifteen minutes into the scrimmage it started to rain, and now, even though we're all wearing cleats, everyone is slipping all over the place. You would think that the coaches would call the game, for safety reasons, but here's the thing: The score is 1-1 and we're playing like this is the World Cup. No joke. I don't know if it's the trying-to-impress-each-other thing or the weather drama or what, but this is a serious game. Everyone's spreading out, passing, following their shots. And it's not as if the guys are going easy on us either. At one point, Kara was flying up the field toward the goal, and this guy Phil slide-tackled her. From then on it was like the gender seal had been broken. Now, it's no holds barred.

I want to score so bad I can taste it.

The problem is, the gold team is playing amazing defense. Lindsey is sweeper, and in practice she barely moves her feet, but today she's like an aerobics instructor, lunging and kicking all over the place. Too bad for Lindsey, I know her weakness: She's a sucker for head fakes. So when Mike Woodmansee sees that I'm open and passes me the ball, there's only one thing on my mind: *Fake left, go right. Fake left, go right.*

I am not thinking about the gold pinny coming up behind me—the one that's getting closer and closer. I am not thinking about it because I just I faked out Lindsey, and the goal is right there, and I am about to take my—

Crap.

I'm flat on my back in the mud, and I don't even know how I got here. All I know is there's someone on top of me.

Who's on top of me? And why the hell isn't he getting—

Oh. A nanosecond.

My. Is all it takes.

God. To realize exactly whose limbs are tangled up with mine.

"Hey," Matt Rigby says. His breath is soft and warm.

There's mud on his chin. And in his hair. He's so close I can literally see his pulse, beating through the vein in his neck.

There are so many things I could say right now.

Hey.

'Sup?

Fancy meeting you here.

Get. Off.

Great game.

Illegal tackle much?

Kiss me.

But when I open my mouth, nothing comes out. Have we been lying here for three seconds or three hours? I don't know. All I know is I don't want to get up. Because this is exactly what it felt like that night on my porch, like the whole world had stopped just for us.

"Nice shot, Jose." Liv is standing over us, grinning.

That's when it hits me. "It went in?"

She nods. "Lower left corner."

"No way." To Matt Rigby I say, "You're cutting off my circulation."

You're cutting off my circulation. I swear to God.

Then, as if that wasn't mortifying enough, he laughs.

"There's something on your face," Bob says. He's squinting up at me, suspicious. "Looks like dirt."

"It's mud," I tell him.

"*Mud?*"

"From soccer practice. Don't worry." I hold out my hands for inspection. "I won't be scooping ice cream with my face."

Bob shudders at the thought.

It's a moot point anyway because summer is over and we've barely had any customers. Mostly what I've been doing when I come to work isn't scooping, it's scrubbing. And hauling FedEx boxes down to the basement. And helping Bob play out his European decorating fantasy—lots of ferns and throw rugs.

"What's *this* thing?" I run my fingers over the shiny silver contraption sitting on the counter.

Bob swats my hand away. "Don't touch!"

"OK!" I jump back. "Sheesh."

"*This,*" he says in a low voice, "is our new cappuccino maker. . . . Observe." He presses a button and a little door pops open. "This is the grinder compartment. Where the espresso beans go." He presses another button and machinery whirs. "See how fast it is? Once the beans are ground"—he whips out a metal cup attached to a black rubber handle—"they go in here. Now . . ." He slides the handled thingy into a slot, clicks it into place, and presses yet a third button, which causes brown liquid to squirt out the bottom. "Voilà!"

"Looks complicated," I say.

"Now we steam the milk."

"There's more?"

"Cappuccino-making is an art, my dear. Art takes time."

"Ah," I say.

I watch as Van Gogh continues his tutorial. When he's finished, he hands me a cheery yellow mug overflowing with froth. "Taste."

"Since when do we have mugs? . . . Wait—is this from one of the mystery boxes in the basement?"

"*Taste.*"

"I'm not really much of a coffee drinker."

Bob huffs a sigh. "Just try it."

"Fine." I take a sip, get a nose full of foam.

"Well?"

"Not bad."

"See?" Bob is smiling, triumphant. Whenever he shows his teeth, I marvel at how tiny they are. Tiny and perfectly square, like a two-year-old's. "Customers are going to love this!"

I am not so sure. "Who drinks cappuccinos with their ice cream?"

Bob shakes his head, exasperated. "There won't *be* any ice cream. We're phasing it out."

"What?"

"Hello? How many European-style cafés do you know that serve ice cream?"

"I don't know," I say. "I've never been to Europe."

Bob purses his lips. "Well. Europe is about to come to you." He tells me to close my eyes.

"Why?"

"Just close them."

What is it with the eye closing around here? First Liv, now Bob. I don't know why people insist on—

"Ta-daaaa!"

He's holding up a wooden sign—yellow with brown lettering and a couple of biscotti painted on—simple, yet elegant. *Fiorello's Café.*

I have to ask, since Bob's last name, I happen to know for a fact, is Schottenstein.

"Please." Bob grimaces. "Schottenstein Café?" He tells me about the year he spent in Italy when he was in his twenties, about the café downstairs from his apartment. "Every morning I would wake to the smell of espresso and pastries. . . . *Fiorello's.* . . . It was heaven." His eyes get misty for a moment. "Best year of my life."

This makes me wonder if there was a girl involved, some Italian beauty he shared his biscotti with. But I don't ask. Because then Bob might feel compelled to tell me the story about how he got his twentysomething heart broken, and I don't want to feel any worse for him than I already do. So instead, I nod.

"Anyway," he says, "I've always wanted to open my own

café. . . . Nobody ever thinks I'll do things, but this time I'm actually doing it." He reaches under the counter, whips out a flyer: FIORELLO'S CAFÉ! GRAND OPENING! "See?"

"Wow," I say. Because he looks so proud of himself right now. And because, even though Bob is a nutcase, he's a nutcase with passion. And that kind of makes me want to root for the guy.

I wake in the middle of the night, sweating.

I had this dream that Matt Rigby came into Fiorello's for a cappuccino, and when he took a sip, his whole head got covered in foam. I kept trying to wipe the foam off him with a towel, but it kept growing back. His mouth would open, trying to tell me something, but I couldn't hear what he was saying because the only thing that came out of his mouth was more foam.

"Spit it out, babe," I kept saying. (God knows why I was calling him "babe." I've never called anyone "babe" in my life.) And anyway, Dream Matt didn't listen to my sage advice. He just kept frothing at the mouth like a rabid squirrel.

Ha! What a stupid dream.

I can't believe I'm still sweating.

Five

THREE WEEKS INTO school, one of the soccer guys announces he's having a party. The whole girls' team is invited. We're all bonded now, apparently. Ever since the scrimmage, it's been fist bumps and high fives in the hallway. Also a lot of jokes about coed naked mud wrestling. From the amount of innuendo in the air, it's obvious there will be hookups on Saturday night, even if no one is coming out and saying it.

In French, Jamie wants to know if I'm going to the party. It's the hundredth time she's asked, and I have yet to provide a straight answer.

"I might be washing my hair," I tell her.

Jamie rolls her eyes and nudges Peter Hersh, as if to say, *Do you believe this loser?*

Peter looks up from his French-English dictionary. "You should go."

I say nothing, leaving Jamie to poke me in the ribs with her pen. "*Hello.* Peter wants you to go."

Peter shakes his head. "I don't care if she goes."

"Thanks a lot," I say.

"Someone else might, though."

Jamie squeals beside me. She's a squealer. "Oh my *God*, Peter, who wants Josie to—"

I reach out my hand to shut her up, but Madame Plouchette beats me to it. "*S'il vous plaît*," she says, rapping Jamie's desk with her ruler. "*Conjugez le verbe 'offusquer' en passé composé.*"

Jamie looks confused. "*Pardonnez-moi?*"

"Pare doan ay muhwa?" Madame gives a pitch-perfect imitation of Jamie's horrendous accent.

Everyone laughs, but Jamie isn't even fazed. She just stands up, tosses her hair, and proceeds to butcher the verb "to annoy."

Someone wants me to go to the party.

Someone. Wants *me.* To go to the party.

The mind boggles.

How is a person supposed to focus on trigonometry?

At the end of soccer practice on Friday, we get the Big Warning from Coach: *Just because you have a bye this weekend doesn't mean you can stay out all night raising Cain, blah, blah, blah.*

I guarantee the boys' team is getting the same lecture. Unlike Wendy Geruntino's purity pledge, the signing of the EHS Athletic Association's Drug and Alcohol Policy is not optional. *Thou Shalt Not Do Jell-O Shots During the Soccer Season* is the point. Zero tolerance.

Coach looks at us through squinty eyes, preparing to lecture some more, but then his mouth twitches at the corner, like he's remembering that he, too, was a teenager once. "All right, ladies," he says. "Bring it in. 'Team,' on three."

Friday nights my mom doesn't have to work. This means two things: movies and junk food. We slide Grandpa Gardner's old leather wing chairs together, kick up our feet on the mosaic coffee table, and pretend we're at the Multiplex. Sometimes Liv joins us, but tonight she's staying home to work on her MyPage. Liv is obsessed with MyPage. She has about five hundred cyber friends, and she's constantly posting new pictures of herself doing weird things: shaving her legs in the rain, juggling kiwis.

So tonight it's just me and my mom, and the movie is *St. Elmo's Fire*—one of the many cheesy '80s movies she has in her collection. We love *St. Elmo's*. It's full of bad hair and heartache, of faithless lovers and secret crushes, of sweaty saxophone players rockin' it out on top of the bar, of cocaine-snorting best friends locking themselves in freezing-cold rooms and having breakdowns, of bitter-sweet endings and fresh beginnings.

There are certain scenes we can quote verbatim. Like the one where Jules and Billy are in the Jeep and she's trying to talk seriously to him, but all he's doing is trying to un-zip her pants. "You break my heart," she says. "Then again, you break everyone's heart." And the camera pans from the Jeep to the house, where Billy's wife is standing on the stoop, holding their baby.

I know a lot of my friends wouldn't be caught dead hanging with their mothers on a Friday night. Some of them, like Schuyler, barely even acknowledge their mom's existence, except to ask for money. Or else they're constantly fighting, like Melanie Jaffin and her mother. I was in the car with them once, and they were having this argument about curfew, and Mel called her mom a bitch. Right to her face. "You. Are such. A bitch."

I can't imagine doing that. Ever. I can honestly say that my mom is my best friend, and even though she gets on my nerves sometimes, she is still one of the kindest, most decent people I know. I just can't imagine a situation where I would slam her like that.

When the movie is over, we polish off a bag of salt-and-vinegar chips, and we talk. We talk about Jonathan, who came back into the store last week and, as I'd predicted, asked my mom out for tomorrow night. We talk about school and soccer and Matt Rigby and mud and cappuccinos and books

and celebrity gossip and the genocide in Darfur and everything under the sun.

That's how it is with us.

After work the next day, I go to Liv's house. I always go to
Liv's on Saturdays because it's my mom's busiest day at the
store. In the morning she has story hour with the little kids;
afternoon is book-of-the-week club; Saturday night is the
poetry slam. Whenever I have a soccer game, my mom will
get one of her assistant managers to cover for her, but today
I don't.

"You smell weird," Liv says. We're sitting on the parquet
floor of her orange bedroom, painting our toenails.

"Thanks a lot," I say, leaning back against one of Liv's
many vintage beanbag chairs. She finds them at tag sales.
The more hideous the color, the better.

"Well, you do," she says. "You smell burnt."

"I *know*. It's the cappuccinos. Bob's obsessed with this
café opening. He made me practice making espresso drinks
all morning. They get into my pores."

"It'll wash off in the shower," she says. "You *are* planning
to take a shower . . ."

I give her arm a little shove.

"Good. Because this is going to be a big night, I can feel
it. We're going to dress you up. Dodd will do your hair. You'll
be like Cinderella! Riggs will take one look at you and—"

"What are you talking about?" I shove her again, harder.

"What? I saw you two at the scrimmage. Everyone did. It's so obvious, Josie."

"Well . . . OK, but that doesn't mean . . . I mean, Peter Hersh could have been talking about someone else wanting me to come tonight. I don't know, that little sophomore winger who's always saying hi to me in the hall. What's his name—Garth? Garrett?"

"Please." Liv laughs. She hands me a bottle of top coat.

"Thanks."

We sit in silence for a minute, finishing our toes. Then I say it. "What if he's an asshole?"

Liv shrugs. "What if he's the love of your life?"

"He *cheated*. On Missy."

"They had an agreement."

"Well," I say. "Maybe."

Liv unweaves the strip of toilet paper from between her toes, holds it to her upper lip. "Hey, who am I? . . . *'Pee and flee, ladies. Pee and flee.'*"

I sigh. "Mr. Charney." Mr. Charney, the hall monitor with the bushy mustache, who likes to stand outside the girls' bathroom between class periods, holding a stopwatch. "Could we focus on me? Please?"

"Yes." Liv uses the toilet paper to wipe a smudge of polish off my big toe. "Now you're perfect."

Suddenly, I have a stroke of genius. "Why don't we go to the movies tonight? There's that new Drew Barrymore playing at—"

"No."

"But you love Drew Barrymore." Fact. There's a poster of Drew Barrymore next to Liv's mirror. Liv blots her lipstick on it. She thinks Drew has great lips.

"Absolutely not," Liv says.

"But—"

"Josie," she says firmly. "We are going to the party, and you are going to face your fears."

"What's that supposed to mean?"

"You're scared of getting hurt, and that's holding you back from doing what you really want to do."

"No, it's not!" (Yes, it is.)

"You can't change what you won't admit."

"OK, Dr. Steve."

"Mock if you must," Liv says, "but Dr. Steve happens to be a very wise person. He's changed a lot of lives for the better."

"I'm sure he has."

"Josie." Liv sighs. "You may not want to hear this, but I'm your best friend, and that means brutal truth, right?"

I nod.

"OK. . . . Matt Rigby is not your dad."

"I *know* that!"

"Do you?"

"Well . . . obviously."

"So stop assuming that every guy in your life is going to do what he did! It's not fair to anyone, least of all you!"

"Wow."

"Sorry. I just had to get that off my chest."

Well.

"OK?" Liv's hand is on my arm, soft and sorrowful. "I just don't want you to sabotage this Riggs thing, you know? . . . Jose?"

"Fine," I say. "Point made."

We stare down at our toes, which are blood red. *Sexy or grisly?* It's hard to tell.

Pops and Dodd drive us to the party. Pops is the disciplinarian in the family—the layer-down of laws—and Dodd is the worrier. Between the two of them, all the parental bases are covered.

"Where exactly are this boy's parents?" Pops asks, almost reprimandingly.

"Who knows?" Liv says. "Aruba? Detroit?" We are side by side in the backseat—Liv in a lime-green flapper dress and cowboy boots, me in jeans and a silver tank top. This is as far as I would go in the outfit department, despite Liv's best efforts.

"Will there be alcohol?" Pops asks.

"Well, it's a party, so . . . yeah."

"I'm not sure I like the sound of this," Dodd murmurs.

"I do," Wyatt pipes in from the other side of Liv. "Why don't you send me along as a bodyguard? Keep these fair maidens safe."

"One beer each," Pops continues, ignoring Wyatt. "No liquor. And absolutely no drugs. Is that understood? Not even pot, because pot is where it all begins."

"Smoke grass," Wyatt quips, "and Pops will kick your ass."

Pops isn't amused. "Wy," he says, "you are not helping. . . . Liv?"

"Aye-aye, Captain," Liv says.

"Josie?"

"Got it," I say.

I know Pops is trying to be a responsible parent, but when he was younger and living in New York City, he was a huge partier. It wasn't until he met Dodd that he stopped going to raves every weekend. Liv and I got the whole story one night when I was sleeping over. Pops and Dodd aren't like other parents. They'll discuss anything—drugs, sex, relationship stuff. No topic is off-limits. Liv and Wyatt can ask whatever they want, and they know they'll get a straight answer.

"You both have your cell phones?" Dodd asks now.

"Yes," we say.

"If anything happens, call. Call *any time*."

Pops pulls up to the house at the same time about fifteen guys are piling out of the SUV in front of us.

Dodd makes a strangled noise in the back of his throat. "Please, *please* don't get in a car with anyone who's been drinking. . . ."

We assure him that we won't and slide out the door before the condom lecture can begin.

"Hey, kids!" Wyatt calls out the window as we're running up the driveway. "We'll be back at eleven thirty! Sharp!"

At the door, Liv reaches out and squeezes my hand, which is already sweating. When I look at her, she smiles. "Your hair looks great."

"You think?" Dodd did some loose-curl thing with hot rollers. It feels weird—like I'm wearing someone else's head.

"Yeah," she says. Then, "Ready?"

"No."

Liv laughs and rings the doorbell.

The Makeup Mafia is already on the dance floor. They wave us over, and Liv starts right in with her signature move: the Flight Attendant. To the beat of the music she stows luggage, points out emergency exits, distributes imaginary drinks.

Some guy in a Viking helmet walks around with a stack of cups and a pitcher of green liquid.

"The punch is *wicked* strong," Schuyler informs us.

From somewhere in the back of the house I can hear the chants. "Chug, chug, chug, chug!" Then, cheers.

Jamie offers me a sip from her cup.

"No, thanks," I say.

"You're so *good*, Josie." She says "good" like it's a bad thing.

Whatever.

I start dancing. I don't love to dance in public, but the lights are dim and the floor is packed, and it's Madonna's *Immaculate Collection* playing—which, come on, how can you not dance to Madonna? At one point we're all voguing away and I spot a clump of varsity jackets across the room. It's like they called one another beforehand: "OK, guys, we're wearing our letterman jackets, right? With jeans? And—"

Oh, God.

Matt Rigby is looking at me.

I see that he's indulged in the hair products tonight. Sweet.

His eyes are locked on mine, and I am still voguing. I know I must look like a moron, since my hands are busy forming geometric shapes in the air around my head, but I would look even more moronic if I stopped. So I keep right on going. On principle.

I can see a little smile tugging at the corner of Matt Rigby's mouth, and I can feel myself start to smile back, and this time I don't even try to stop it from happening. Because maybe Liv is right. Maybe what I need to do is loosen up and let fate take its course. Maybe this seven-month "thing" between us really is meant to—

Well. Just shoot me now.

There she is: the redheaded cheerleader. Hanging on to Matt's arm like she owns him, whispering in his ear.

I feel sick. I haven't had a single drink, and already I want to throw up.

I turn around to grab Liv, but she's not on the dance floor. She's not even in the room.

How does a person just *disappear* at a party? That's my question. I've searched everywhere, even the bedrooms, which of course are full of random, punch-infused hookups, and, which, come to think of it, I don't know why I bothered checking. A) Liv never has more than one drink, and B) not in a million years would she deign to hook up with a high-school guy.

But I need to find her, and that means looking everywhere.

I head outside. On the back lawn a bunch of guys are playing soccer in the dark, and they're killing themselves laughing because they keep falling down.

"Hey," I call out. "Have you guys seen Liv?"

"Who?" someone calls back.

"Olivia! Weiss-Longo!"

"She's hot!" another guy yells.

Someone wolf whistles, and I'm about to yell something else, but a hand has just grabbed mine.

I know, even before I turn around. Matt Rigby has the warmest hands.

"Hey," he says low.

Every hair on my neck stands at attention.

"Did you check your cell?" he asks.

"What?"

"Check your cell. Maybe she texted you."

"Why would she? . . . Fine." I try to yank my hand back, but he just holds on tighter. I have to reach into my pocket from the opposite side, which is annoying, but then I flip open my phone and there it is:

J, wnt 4 ride. Wll xplain L8r. B bck 11:29. Hv fn 2nite!!!
xo, L

I stand there, staring at the message.

"Everything OK?"

I don't know if it is, but I nod and slip the phone back in my pocket.

"Hey." Matt Rigby steers my elbow to turn me around, and I let him.

"Hey what?" I say.

We're facing each other now, and he's holding both my hands in his, and they are so warm. Then there's the smell of him—part beer, part deodorant, part I don't know what . . . leaves? For a moment, all I want to do is breathe.

"Why are you avoiding me?" he asks.

"I'm not avoiding you."

"Every time I see you, you run the other way."

"No I don't."

My eyes have adjusted to the dark now, and I can see him smile. "Come on. Admit it."

"Every time I see *you*, you've got your own personal cheering section."

"What?"

"Nothing."

"Wait—Tessa?"

"I don't know, Matt. Is that her name? I can't seem to keep track of your girlfriends."

He laughs, as though I've just told the cleverest of jokes.

"I'm glad you think this is funny," I say.

"Tessa's not my girlfriend," he says. "She's just a friend. For the record."

"Ah," I say, nodding. "You guys must have one of those 'agreements' you're so fond of." I can hear the snottiness of my tone, and I hate it, but I can't help myself.

Riggs is silent for a moment. Then he says, "I knew it."

"What?"

He takes a breath. "I knew you thought I was lying that night, about Missy. That I was just saying what I said to hook up with you. But I wasn't."

"Uh-huh," I say. I'm focused on his eyes. I once read that you can tell if someone's lying by how much they blink, or if they glance to the side, but he's not doing either. His eyes are locked on mine.

"The thing with Missy and me was . . . complicated."

"Complicated how?" I say.

"It was like this arranged marriage thing. We've known each other forever. Our parents are best friends, and they always wanted us to, you know, get together, and Missy was really into it, but I was never exactly . . ." He hesitates. "Before she left for college I finally told her I was into . . . you know . . . someone else."

He's squeezing both my hands, and it takes me a second to realize—he means me! Then I remember where we are, and I have to ask: "How drunk are you?"

He shakes his head. "I'm not."

"You smell like beer."

"*Half* a beer. Just to get my courage up."

"For what?"

"This," he says. He leans in and kisses me, soft and slow, and it's as if our mouths were made just to come together, and now his hands are on my back, pressing me closer, and I can't believe everything that's flying through my head in this one moment. New Year's and porch swings and dreams and mud and fireworks and *St. Elmo's* and prom and cheesy song lyrics and . . . and I'm pushing him away . . . why am I pushing him away?

Matt reaches for my arm to pull me back. "What's wrong?"

I shake my head. "Nothing. Just . . . I can't do this if you're going to mess with my head."

He's quiet for a second, like he's searching for the right words. Then he says them: "I'm not. I won't."

"How do you know?"

"I know."

"How?"

"I've wanted this since tenth grade. Ever since I saw you do that peer-ed skit in assembly. The one about cigarettes."

"Yeah, right." I'm rolling my eyes like I don't believe him. But I'm kind of tingling, too.

"You were wearing a fuzzy blue sweater. And your hair was all twisty. Kind of like . . ." He reaches out and gathers my hair into a pile on top of my head. "With a pencil sticking out of it."

"You remember that?"

"Scout's honor," he says, holding up three fingers. "Your skit was very convincing. I haven't smoked since."

I try to suppress the urge to call him a big dork, but as usual my mouth has other plans. "You're such a dork," I say. Then I touch my hand to his arm, to show him I mean it in the best possible way.

"*I'm* a dork?" he says, smiling. "*Me*?" He takes a step back, and then, out of nowhere, he starts singing. *"Come on, Vogue! Let your body groove to the music! Hey, hey, hey!"*

It takes about two seconds for all the guys who were playing soccer to gather around us on the deck, clapping and cheering as Matt Rigby's hands form geometric shapes in the air around his head. And despite the fact that he's mocking my dance moves, I have to laugh. Because he looks so ridiculous, and because his eyes haven't left mine, and because now he's reaching out his hand for me to join him, and I am actually doing it.

Here we are: voguing side by side in the cool September air, sober, to absolutely no music. I can just see the word "dork-out" hanging in the air above us.

Also the word "us."

"Get a room!" someone from the peanut gallery yells, and instead of being embarrassed, Matt Rigby pulls me in and kisses me. Right there, in front of everyone. How this is happening is beyond me. I only wish Liv were here to see it.

Eleven thirty-two p.m., the backseat of Dodd's car. Two things are going on: the parental inquisition and stealth texting.

>**Pops:** "How was the party?"
>**Us:** "Great."

>**Me:** Whr wr u?
>**Liv:** Lng stry. GR8 guy.
>**Me:** Wht??? Who???

>**Dodd:** "How many fingers am I holding up?"
>**Us:** "Three."
>**Dodd:** "Good."

Liv: Finn. He gos 2 UMass. We mt on MyPg.

Me: W8. Whn did ths hppn???

Liv: IDK. 2 wks ago?

Pops: "Any bodily harm?"

Us: "No."

Dodd: "Any heartbreak?"

Us: "No."

Liv: Enuf me. U. How ws ur nite?

Me: OMG. Whr 2 bgin? . . .

All the way back to my house, we text so furiously, it's amazing our phones don't explode. After we say our good-byes I sprint up my front steps, fully amped, prepared to tell my mom everything. I'm ready for the couch, the popcorn, the whole heart-to-heart, mother-daughter, let-it-all-hang-out thing that happens every time I come home from a party.

Except for this time.

This time is something else entirely.

Try walking into your living room to find your mother tangled up on the couch with some guy she just met, her shirt bunched up around her neck. Try clearing your throat and watching them pop up, grinning like a couple of bobblehead dolls and frantically adjusting their clothes. Try reminding yourself of who is the teenager in this scenario and who is the parent, without actually saying, *Oh my GOD, Mother, did you WANT me to see this?!*

I know. I was the one who encouraged her. I was the one who said, *Put yourself out there*, who told her how cute Jonathan was, that I was happy he asked her out. But now, watching the whole thing unfold in my living room, I feel like—OK, this is going to sound completely juvenile, but it's true—I feel like the cheese in "The Farmer in the Dell." *The cheese stands alone.* When Jonathan stands up to introduce himself, what I really want to say is, "*I'm* not the cheese. *You're* the cheese."

Instead, I make my head nod. *Uh-huh, uh-huh. Nice to meet you, too*, while my mom stands between us, smiling. She gestures to the couch and says, "Josie, sit. Tell us about the party."

"Nothing to tell." It almost hurts to say this, but I do. "My night was totally uneventful."

Normally my mom would know I'm lying and call me on it.

Not this time.

"Well," I say. "I'm beat . . . I guess I'll go up."

She hugs me when I say this, relieved that I read her mind. When she says to me, "Good night, sweetheart," it's actually code: *Thanks, sweetheart. For heating it.*

ſix

JONATHAN IS A *jazz aficionado.*

This is what my mother tells me over breakfast. Latin jazz, soul jazz, jazz fusion—you name it, he knows it. Jazz is the reason he became a music teacher. My mom recounts a story he told her last night, about the first time he heard Eddie "Lockjaw" Davis (whoever that is) play the saxophone.

"He *cried,*" she tells me, one hand patting her chest. "He was twelve years old and he was so moved by the music, he actually *wept.*"

"Wow," I say.

"Can you imagine?"

Yes, actually, I can. I can imagine him getting shoved into a locker by the junior-high football team.

"Syrup?" my mom says.

I nod, take the bottle.

It's waffles this morning. Waffles that feature an assortment of dried fruit—apricots, raisins, dates—which give them an oddly diseased appearance.

Jonathan is a Samaritan.

This is the next thing she tells me. One weekend a month he volunteers at North Haven Hospital, doing art projects with terminally ill kids. Friendship bracelets, decoupage, quilts. . . .

My mother goes on and on, and I don't want to burst her heart-shaped bubble, but it sounds to me like Jonathan is trying awfully hard to impress her. Ridiculously hard. *Obscenely* hard.

"What's next?" I ask. "Leaping tall buildings in a single bound?"

"Well, he *was* a high-jumper in college."

"I was kidding."

"I know." My mom laughs, delighted. "I know! He sounds too good to be true, right?"

I shoot her a look that says, *Exaggeration of the century much?*—which she either ignores or doesn't catch.

"I can't believe this is happening," is what she says now, sounding every inch the enamored schoolgirl. She even looks the part: blue eyes shining, cheeks abloom.

OK. I should be happy to see my mother happy. And I am. I *am*. It's just, one minute she's busting out the old Paul Tucci yearbook, and the next—

"So, I invited him for dinner."

"What?" I put down my fork. "When?"

"Tonight."

"But it's Sunday."

"And?"

"And the Weiss-Longos are coming. It's our turn to host."

"I'm sure the Weiss-Longos won't mind if Jonathan joins us," she says.

"No, it's just . . . you just *met* the guy, like three weeks ago. Don't you think it's a little soon to be—"

"What? Excited about someone?" My mom puts down her fork, frowns. "It's not like this happens to me every day, Josie. It doesn't. I've had—what—six dates in sixteen years?"

I can see the hurt in her face, and I feel horrible. I tell her that Jonathan seems like a good guy, and I want her to be happy.

"Thank you," she says. "He *is* a good guy. A really decent, what-you-see-is-what-you-get kind of person."

"Yes," I say.

It doesn't take a genius to read between my mother's lines: *Jonathan is the antithesis of Paul Tucci. Good. Decent. Not a heartbreaker.*

"You deserve it," I say.

She nods. Then she says, "I think I'll make steak. What guy doesn't like steak, right? And some kind of potato?"

"Sure," I say.

"OK. Steak it is."

Her face has smoothed out again. She's back to normal. For a second I consider telling her about last night—about

Matt Rigby and the kiss, and Liv—but she's already whipping out the cookbooks. She's starting a shopping list: *Filet mignon. Flowers. Wine.*

I go upstairs with a pit in my stomach, and I don't even know why it's there, but I'm actually glad the café opening is today, so I can focus my mind on that instead of on my mother's new boyfriend.

Fiorello's looks amazing. Funky art and plush couches, glass-topped tables, ferns. Some little elf has been working over-time, unloading FedEx boxes. And the *smell*. Bob doesn't do anything half-assed; he hired two gourmet bakers for the opening. The air smells sugary and yeasty, and the display cases—the ones that used to hold ice cream—are now full of pastries.

"You need a taste tester," I tell Bob. I reach for the sliding glass door. "You know, just to make sure . . ."

"No sampling!" He swats my hand away.

"Fine." I shrug. "Poison the customers. See if I care."

Bob's brow crinkles.

"*Kidding,*" I say. "I'm kidding."

"I'm sorry." He grabs a towel and begins buffing the already-shiny countertops. "We open in forty-two minutes. I'm nervous."

Nervous, obsessive, manic . . .

"Don't worry," I tell him. "Everything will be fine."

✳   ✳   ✳

By Elmherst standards, this place is rocking. Wherever Bob posted those flyers, they worked. There must be twenty customers in here.

"We need more of those little tube-y things," I tell Meg, the college student who usually works the shifts I can't. Bob scheduled everyone to work today, which is making the space behind the counter feel even tighter than normal.

"Cannoli." Meg hands me a tray of tube-y things. "*God.* These people are like *vultures* with the free samples."

Bob winds his way through the crowd with a platter of biscotti and mini coffees. His cheeks are flushed pink, and the fringe of hair around his bald spot is frizzing out from the humidity.

"These biscotti are to die for," a woman says, reaching out for Bob's arm with her long, manicured fingertips. Bob ducks his head to the side, loving the compliment—also, clearly, trying to avoid the transfer of germs.

"We need more steamed milk." Drake, the kid with the zits who works Friday nights, shoves a pitcher in my face.

"Bob didn't show you how to do it?"

Drake rolls his eyes. "He doesn't like my foam. He says it's too flat."

"Here," I say. "Take the register. I'll steam."

I sashay past Drake and past the baker who's sliding a tray of cookies out of the oven. They're the almond variety, rich and buttery, with little nut slivers on top. Breathing in, I feel a burst of spit fill my mouth, reminding me that

I'm famished. I never did finish my waffle this morning. I was too distracted by the Jonathan discussion to eat.

Jazzy Jonathan.

Coming for dinner.

Tonight.

Ach.

OK, I'm not going to focus on that. I'm going to focus on milk-steaming. And bean-grinding. And assembling beautiful, fluffy, cinnamon-dappled cappuccinos for the masses—

"Excuse me, young lady?"

I turn. "Yes?"

The man is silver-haired, with square shoulders and a wide, ruddy face. He smiles at me and I suddenly realize who he is and give a little jump. Naturally, the pitcher of scalding milk in my hand jumps, too. And sloshes onto the front of my shirt. And soaks through to my bare skin.

"Oh, shit!" I announce, trying to pull the fabric of my shirt away from my scalding chest. "Hot! Hot shit!"

Paul Tucci's father's eyes widen, and he points to the sink behind me. "Water! Cold water!"

In moments like these, you don't think about decorum. You don't think at all. You just spring across the floor like a jungle cat and stick your entire torso under the faucet, letting the cold water run, and run, and run.

"Oh . . . my . . ." Liv is laughing so hard she's gasping for breath. "God! . . . Hot! . . ." Tears are literally streaming down her face. "Hot shit!"

"Thank you," I say. "Thank you so much for laughing at my humiliation. Really. I feel so much better now."

"I'm ... sorry. ... It's just ... you *burned* ... your ..." A fresh fit of giggles erupts and Liv collapses face-first on the bed.

"That's right, Olivia," I say. "I burned my boobs. Hilarious! Keep it up."

We are in my room. Everyone else is downstairs, mingling and drinking wine. Preparing to eat my mother's steak. Already I can tell how this night will go: about as well as the rest of my day. It would be nice to have a best friend who appreciated the gravity of the situation.

"You know," I say, "for someone who dates college guys, you're awfully immature."

Suddenly, amazingly, Liv rolls over and sits up. "Guy. Singular. And I wouldn't call it 'dating.' More like . . ."

"What?"

"Hanging out. Hooking up. *You* know."

I do know. You can't be friends with Liv and not know exactly where she stands on the subject of sex: i.e., it's a magnificent thing. One time last year, she got into a half-hour-long morality debate with Wendy Geruntino in the middle of the cafeteria. Wendy's logic consisted of, *God wants us to stay pure for marriage*, and Liv's argument was, *Hey, God made us sexual creatures. If he wanted teenagers to wait that long, he would have made puberty start at twenty-five.*

And don't even get Liv started on the double standard.

She'll give you an earful: *If a guy wants to have sex, he's a stud, right? If a girl wants to have sex, she's a slut, a ho, a trollop. How warped is that?*

"Well," I say now. "I hope you're using protection."

"Of course," she says firmly. "I'm a safety girl. . . . But we weren't talking about me."

"Actually, we were."

"No, we weren't."

"Well, I'd rather talk about you."

"We can talk about me after you tell me the rest of the story."

"There *is* no rest of the story."

"So, what—you just stayed there, cooling off your boobs in the sink, and that's it? You didn't talk to him at all?"

"Nope."

Liv shakes her head.

"Well, what was I supposed to do?"

"Gee, I don't know, Josie. Offer him a pastry? Crack a joke? *Something* to get the ball rolling?"

"And what ball might that be?"

Liv heaves a sigh.

"What?" I say.

"Josie, they live fifteen miles away from you. We have the address to prove it. And I don't care what you call them, they *are* your grandparents. Don't you even want to *try* to get to know them?"

No, I think. *I already had grandparents. Maybe they never lived in a mansion or went to some Ivy League college, but at least they were there for me.*

"Do you have any idea how lucky you are that this is happening?" Liv says. "There are people who try for years to find family members. *Decades*, even. Dr. Steve had this show once, and this girl—"

"Please," I say. "Not Dr. Steve."

"I'm just saying, if I were you—"

"But you're not."

"But if I *were*—"

"But you're *not*, Liv, OK? You're not me!" I realize I'm yelling and lower my voice. "Just . . . you don't know how I feel about this. . . . *I* don't know how I feel about this. OK?"

Liv grimaces. "OK. Sorry."

"It's OK." I sit down on the bed next to her. "My mom would wig, if she knew."

"Are you going to tell her?"

"I don't know yet."

Liv raises her eyebrows, but I don't elaborate.

Because there is my mother's voice, calling from downstairs.

The steak is ready.

Here's what a fly on the wall would think: *Gosh, what a lovely dinner party. Lovely food, lovely conversation, lovely people, everyone getting along, no painful or awkward moments. Overall, a solid B-plus evening.*

Here's what I am thinking: *Is it bedtime yet?* I'm sitting at the table, watching my mom and Jonathan make goo-goo eyes at each other, and all I want to do is evaporate from the dining room.

Which makes me feel like a jerk. A horrible daughter. Because the fact of the matter is, Jonathan is a nice guy. Perfectly nice! Nice-looking, nice manners. When Wyatt mentions he's a Red Sox fan, Jonathan says the nicest possible thing: "I've got season tickets. Name your game, and they're yours." But seeing Jonathan reach out and take my mother's hand between bites of apple pie makes me want to poke him with a fork.

I'm sorry, but it's true.

It takes every ounce of restraint in my body not to yell across the table, *You just met!*

Later, lying in bed, I feel like crap. I tell myself that tomorrow I will try harder: give Jonathan a chance, for my mom's sake.

And while I'm at it, I should probably tell her about seeing Paul Tucci's dad and the whole moved-back thing. Maybe she'll say, "Ah, well, how nice for them." Better yet, "The Tuccis are ancient history, Josie. I've moved on. I've got Jonathan now."

I don't think that's what she'll say, but who knows? I should at least give her the information. Then she can do what she wants with it.

ſeven

SIX THIrTY a.m. and my mother is MIA. All
I see is a yellow Post-it, stuck next to a carton of juice on the
counter.

> *J-Bear,*
> *Jonathan and I went for a run.*
> *He made granola!*
> *Help yourself!*
> *Love, Mom*

Which means one of two things: either he woke up at the
crack of dawn to get here, or he slept over.
Well.
OK, this is none of my business. They're consenting

adults. And anyway, it's kind of a relief not to be having the Big Debriefing about last night's dinner and how great it was. In fact, I don't have to talk at all. Not like every other morning when my mom is firing questions at me about school or soccer or "the boy" or Liv or my deepest, most intimate feelings or any of that other crap that mothers love to bond over with their daughters right when they wake up.

For the first time in my life, I can eat breakfast in peace. Which is actually kind of nice. Yes, it is.

"Who *makes* granola, anyway?" I ask Liv on the bus.

"I don't know," she says. "Nature lovers?"

I snort.

"Why does it bother you?"

"It doesn't bother me."

"I thought you liked Jonathan."

"I do. Jonathan is . . . fine."

"OK," she says slowly. "So, what's the problem?"

"I don't know. I don't know! It's just . . . happening too fast."

"In what way? Wait—" She pushes my arm. "Did he stay over last night?"

I shake my head. Then I nod. "I think so."

"Go, Kate!"

"Don't say that!"

"Why? He's hot."

"This is my *mother* we're talking about."

"So? Your mother doesn't deserve a sex life?"

I take a quick breath in, then say, "We are not talking about this."

Liv shrugs, rustles around in her bag for her cell phone, and starts punching buttons.

"I mean, just because you're all gung-ho casual sex—"

She stops. "I am not all *gung-ho casual sex.*"

"No? So you're not texting your boy toy right now?"

"His name is Finn," she says, a bit sharply.

Finn. What kind of name is that, anyway? Whatever happened to normal names like Mike and Joe?

We sit in silence while she turns away, pressing buttons like mad. Then, just as we're pulling up to school, she clicks her phone shut and looks at me. "Do you want your mom to be happy?"

"Of course."

"Does she seem happy with Jonathan?"

"Well . . . so far."

"Then give the guy a chance, Josie!"

"I'm trying!" I say.

I walk off the bus with a sick taste in my mouth. I think it's the granola, trying to get out.

There's a lot of whispering in homeroom. Some snickering. Also, high fives and thumps on the back for Peter Hersh, who, according to the Saturday night rumor mill, spent some quality time in the shower with a freshman field hockey player named Amber.

"Oh my God," Kimmy Gustofson says, leaning forward and breathing hot bubble-gum breath in my face. "Josie. How *was* it?"

I unzip my backpack, pull out my binder. "What?"

"The *party*," Lorelei Hill says, pulling her chair in close. "On Saturday. We heard it was *out* of control."

Kimmy lowers her voice an octave. "Did Jamie Mann really give Kyle Longbreak a . . . *you* know . . . in the hot tub?"

"*What?*" I say.

"A blow—"

"*No!*"

Truthfully, I have no idea what Jamie did or didn't do this weekend, but I'm not about to add heat to the hot tub. And anyway, Wendy Geruntino, who sits in front of Kimmy, has turned around and is giving us the most distressed look. "I'm sad, listening to you."

"Then don't," Lorelei says.

"I'm sorry," Wendy says. "It's just, hearing about all these casual, meaningless physical encounters—it makes me think, where's the respect? Where's the honor? The—"

"This is *homeroom*," Kimmy says with a snort, "not Bible study."

"Ladies! Earth to the ladies in the back. . . ."

I turn my attention to Mr. Catenzaro, glad that the conversation is over. It would only be a matter of time before the subject turned from Jamie Mann and Kyle Longbreak to me and—

Oh. Kimmy has passed me a note.

You and Matt Rigby???

Suddenly, my tongue feels like sandpaper. Suddenly, my Saturday night feels just as casual and meaningless as all the other grist for the rumor mill.

I shake my head, write back: *False.* And wait for the bell to ring, so I can be three minutes closer to the end of this day.

First period is no better. I have chemistry, and for me chemistry is already a nightmare. Those formulas that Ms. Monty writes on the board might as well be Japanese for all the sense they make. Then there are the labs. Today it's something with hydrogen sulfide, which would be nauseating enough because it smells like rotten eggs, but then add this: My lab partner is Ron Mullaney, one of the guys who was playing soccer at the party.

I am waiting—just waiting—for a comment.

"We need safety goggles for this one," Ron says, reading from the lab manual. "And gloves. H_2S is, like, extremely toxic. . . . Josie?"

He's looking at me. Great. Well, let him say whatever he needs to say about Saturday night. I can take it.

"Josie."

"What?"

He points to the box in front of me. "Goggles."

"Oh," I say. "Right."

I put on my safety gear, and we start the experiment. Ron mutters to himself the whole time, making little notes on our lab card as he goes. The smell is horrendous. I have to cover my face with my sweatshirt just to breathe.

At one point, Ron turns to me. "You don't like chemistry, do you?"

"Why do you say that?"

"Just a sense."

"Sorry," I say. Then, "Do you want me to write the lab report?"

He shrugs. "I'm basically done."

"Sorry," I say again. I meant *sorry* for slacking, but now something else flies out of my mouth—the kind of thing you wish you could hold back, but you can't: "I know I made an ass of myself at the party."

Ron blinks, confused.

"On the deck," I say. "Dancing? And . . . you know . . ."

"Right." Something flashes across Ron's face, like a grimace. "Well, don't worry about it. We all do stupid stuff at parties."

"Yeah," I mutter, closing my binder and shoving it in my backpack. "It was stupid."

"Seriously," Ron says firmly. "Don't even think about it. A lot of girls do a lot crazier things at parties. . . . Anyway, you know Riggs. . . ."

I wait for some elaboration. Any elaboration.

But it doesn't come.

I know Riggs what? I know Riggs: He's always making out on decks? I know Riggs: He likes crazy girls? I know Riggs . . . I *don't* know Riggs. That much is perfectly clear. I don't know Riggs at all.

Between fourth and fifth periods, I'm winding my way through the junior corridor. As usual, it's mayhem, full of shouts and banging metal. Normally I wouldn't mind, but today it seems louder than ever. Also oppressively hot. In gym class, Mrs. Blackburn made us jump rope for half an hour, and I am still sweating. I stop and lean my cheek against the tile wall for a moment. Because it's cool, soothing. *Ahhhh.* I could stay here for the rest of the day.

But then Bob's voice pops into my head. Mr. Germ-a-phobe: *Do you know how many billions of bacteria infest the average surface of a public building? Do you know how many billions of microorganisms enter the pores of your skin through contact alone?*

No, Bob, I don't. But, hey, thanks for the paranoia.

The crowd is thinning out. Luckily my next class is

only two doors down from my locker. My locker, which is right—

Oh.

Blue polo shirt.

Blond hair curling over the collar.

Jeans.

Matt Rigby is standing in front of my locker, looking straight at me. For a moment I'm not sure what to do, but I need my French binder because I'm on my way to French. I have no choice but to stop.

"Hey, Josie."

"Hey."

I don't trust myself to say anything else, so I leave it at that.

"What do you have now?"

"French."

We stand there. Just looking at each other, not moving.

"I'll walk you. I have Spanish, so we're heading the same way. . . ."

"OK."

He steps aside to let me open my locker, and I have to will my hand not to shake as I turn the lock.

I'm racking my brains for something clever to say. He's standing so close, I can smell his gum. Juicy Fruit.

"You don't have to walk me," I tell him, shoving my French binder into my backpack.

"I want to."

"Why?"

He pretends to think for a moment. Then, a little smile plays at the corner of his mouth. "You can't ignore me if I'm walking next to you."

"Why would I do that?"

"I don't know . . . people are saying stuff. I thought you might be regretting our little . . . dance-off."

I shrug. "Everyone says stuff after parties."

I can't believe how calm I sound.

As we walk down the hall, a million tiny lightning bugs flicker around my stomach. When we make it to the French room, we stop. Matt Rigby turns to me, and his face is serious, and I know he's about to say something devastating. He's going to say that Saturday night was fun, but he doesn't want me to get the wrong idea. He doesn't want to lead me on.

We are directly in front of the door, blocking it, and we have to move for Peter Hersh to get through.

"'Sup, Riggs."

"'Sup, Hershy."

It's weird how guys do that—call each other by their last names. But I kind of like the fact that Riggs is *Riggs*, and not just *Matt* like all the other Matts in this school. Matt Dineen. Matt Leone. Matt—

"Josie."

"Yeah." I focus on his chin, not his eyes.

"I had a great time on Saturday."

I look up. "What?"

"I had a great time. With you. At the party."

"Yeah?"

"Yeah."

He's smiling, and I can feel a ridiculous grin spreading across my face too. We must look like a couple of idiots.

The final bell rings, and I don't know why, but we're not moving.

"And just so you know," Matt Rigby says, "I've been practicing my dance moves."

"Oh, *really*."

"Yes, really."

"That's funny," I say, "because I have too. In fact, I've been getting *really* good. I've been reading *Dancing for Dummies*, you know, for technique. . . ."

He laughs. I can see the Juicy Fruit on his tongue, a tiny gray wad, and I have the strange desire to reach out and touch it.

"So, maybe we'll have a rematch sometime," he says.

"Maybe we will."

Before we can say anything else, there's a sound at the door. It's Madame Plouchette, tapping the glass with her pointer and frowning.

Matt reaches out, squeezes my hand. "You are so busted."

I squeeze back. "Yup."

Madame will probably humiliate me in front of everyone. She'll make me conjugate some embarrassing verb.

But right now, I don't even care. All I can do is smile.

I'm in the cafeteria, eating mac and cheese with the girls,
when Riggs walks by on his way to the guys' soccer table. He
doesn't stop so much as brush his fingers against my neck as
he goes.

Now I have goose bumps.

Liv yanks me up and pulls me over to the water fountain,
away from Jamie and Kara and Schuyler, who are too busy
gossiping to notice. "What was *that*?" Liv asks.

And I tell her about my morning.

"So, it's happening," she says. "You and Riggs."

"I guess," I say quietly. "I don't know."

"*I* know," Liv says. Not quietly.

I shrug.

Liv heaves a sigh. "Finally."

"OK. What about you? And Finn?"

"We're having a good time. It's, like, somewhat casual,
but it's only been a few weeks, you know? And college guys
operate differently. So, we'll see. . . . I'm taking it day by
day."

"Yeah," I say. "Me too."

Liv smiles. I smile. For a second I feel hope for us. Her
and Finn; me and Riggs. The details of how we will all live

happily ever after I'm not too clear about, but the hope part
is there.

Right before soccer I check my cell and there's a message
from my mom. She wants me to call her. I go into one of the
bathroom stalls and dial Twilight Books.

"Mom," I say low. "I have to tell you something. . . . I
kissed Matt Rigby."

"You did?"

"Yes! At the party. It was really weird, how it happened.
At first, I thought he was with this girl Tessa, this cheerleader, but it turns out—"

"I'm sorry, honey," my mom says, cutting me off. "Hold
on a sec." Things get muffled in the background. "It's Josie,"
I hear her say. There's a lot of murmuring. Then she says
to me, "I'm sorry, what were you saying? Tessa, the cheerleader?"

"Who were you talking to?" I say.

"Jonathan."

"Doesn't he have to work? I thought he was a music
teacher."

"He is. He took the day off. . . . Tell me about Matt—"

"He took the day *off*, to hang out at the *bookstore*?"

"Yes. . . . So—"

"Huh," I say.

In an instant, she seems to forget what we were talking

about and launches into how Jonathan asked her to go to the
movies with him tonight—some German film playing at the
arts cinema in town. They thought they'd grab a bite at that
new bistro on Broad Street—

"So, go," I say.

"You don't mind?"

"Why would I mind?"

"So . . . can you get a—"

"Ride home? Yeah. I'll hitchhike from work. I'll eat biscotti for dinner. Whatever."

"You sound irritated."

"I'm not *irritated*. I don't care if you go out. I just . . .
maybe next time you could give me a little advance notice.
Maybe I would make other plans for my night."

"Josie."

"*What?*"

She's quiet for a second. Then she says, "Do you want to
join us?"

"I have a *job*, Mom."

"We could go to a late show. . . ."

"It's a *school* night," I say. "I have *homework*." Then,
"Look, I have to go. I'm late for practice."

"OK. . . . So, you're really OK with tonight?"

"Asked and answered."

After we say good-bye I snap my phone shut so hard I
drop it. It almost lands in the toilet, which would be very

poetic. Because I'm pissed. Even though I know I have no right to be, I am. I just am.

I shove the phone in my duffel and sprint out to the field. I hope Coach makes us run the entire practice. I'll go for hours. I'll run and run and run and run, until I stop feeling this way. Until I'm numb.

Eight

SEVEN FIFTEEN P.M., and we have cus-
tomers. Incredibly. At Bananarama we hardly ever had customers on Monday nights, but Fiorello's is hopping. There
must be twelve, fifteen people in here, and I'm determined
not to spill anything. Or burn anything. Or drop anything.
Or otherwise upset Bob's exquisite order of things. He wasn't
exactly pleased with the boob-scalding incident, so I am doing what I can to redeem myself.

My cappuccinos are improving. My foam is as fluffy as
cumulus clouds. I'm working on a mixture of chocolate shavings and nutmeg for toppings when I hear a deep voice from
the other end of the counter. "What's good tonight?"

I look up and my stomach jumps, but thankfully the rest
of me stays where it is.

"Sorry to startle you," Paul Tucci's father says. "*Again.*"

He's grinning, a flash of straight white teeth. Dentures, I am thinking. They're too perfect to be real. Dentures that sleep in a jelly jar on his bedside table, which is dressed in a doily crocheted by Paul Tucci's mother.

I can feel my eyelid start to twitch.

"Are you recovered?" he asks. "From . . . last time?"

I nod, my face heating up. Where is Bob? He's supposed to be here, working the pastry shelves while I make drinks. I look around, but he's nowhere to be seen. . . .

"Nico Tucci," Mr. Tucci says, extending one hand. "Call me Big Nick. Everyone else does." His fingers are thick, hairy at the knuckles. His watch is gold with a cracked leather strap.

"Um," I say. His hand is huge compared to mine—huge and warm, with a ridge of calluses across the palm. "Josie."

I don't say my last name. I *can't* say my last name.

My eyelid is twitching like crazy.

"Josie," he repeats. "Nice. . . . So, what do you recommend tonight, Josie?"

"Uh. . . . I recommend the uh . . ." I can just see my freshman-year speech teacher, Mrs. Ostenek, shaking her permed head.

I am about to tell him I like the almond cookies when Bob comes gliding up behind me.

"The crumiri," he says smoothly, "those little crescent-shaped ones, are excellent. Baked fresh this afternoon."

"Great." Big Nick smacks his hands together. "I'll take six."

Bob nods approvingly and begins plucking cookies off their tray, placing them in a white bakery box. "Josie," he says low.

"Yeah."

Bob frowns, jutting his head in the direction of the coffee bar.

"Oh," I say. "Right!" I turn to Big Nick and say, in precisely the manner I have been instructed, "May I interest you in a beverage? A cappuccino, perhaps? We also have a fine assortment of gourmet teas. . . ."

Paul Tucci's father raises both eyebrows, as though to say, *You're a very strange young lady.*

If I were watching me, I'd be saying the same thing.

But now he is smiling and asking if we have hot cocoa.

We do, of course. And I say, "Would you like whipped cream with that?"

"I can't believe he came in again," I tell Liv on the phone. I'm calling from the PVTA—the public bus—which I had no choice but to ride home.

"Maybe he'll become a regular," Liv says. "Your best customer."

"Thanks, but no thanks."

"But you could get to know him. Not as a grandfather, just as a regular guy. It's a golden opportunity, Jose."

I snort.

Liv ignores me and keeps going. "OK, so what are you going to tell Kate?"

"Nothing," I say.

"Nothing," she repeats.

"She's way into this Jonathan thing."

"And your point is . . ."

"My point is she's at a *German film* tonight. Since when does my mother watch movies with subtitles?"

"People evolve."

"Exactly. She's *evolved*. Beyond the Tucci thing. . . . Well, OK, maybe not *evolved*. But let's just say she's *transitioned* to Jonathan. . . . Anyway, she doesn't need to hear about this."

"Your call," Liv says.

"That's right," I tell her. "My call."

When I get home, I phone Liv again. "She's not back yet," I say. "Should I be worried?"

"No," Liv says. "It's only nine thirty. And it's a hot date."

"It is not a *hot date*."

"Fine. A cold date. It's still early."

"You're right."

"I know."

"Are you freaked, being there alone? Do you want Dodd

to come and pick you up? I'd do it myself, but I still have three weeks until my license test. . . ."

"That's OK."

"You sure?"

"Yeah. I have a ton of homework to do. Anyway, she won't be too late."

"Unless he takes her *parking* after the movie."

I groan. "Please."

"What, you think no one over the age of eighteen hooks up in a car? What about that movie where the mom and dad are in the minivan and he's all stressed about work, so she unbuckles her seatbelt, right there on the highway, and gives him a—"

"Liv," I say, cutting her off. "Do me a favor."

"What?"

"Stop talking about my mother and hooking up in the same sentence. Or the same paragraph."

"You mean you don't want to think of your mother as a physical being, with physical needs."

"That's what I mean."

"You know that's warped, right?"

"I don't care."

"If you ever have sex, Josie, you'll see the world in a whole new way. Believe me."

"Maybe you should try thinking about something else for a change. Get your head out of the gutter."

Liv laughs.

After I hang up the phone I go into the kitchen for something to eat. I stare into the refrigerator for a long time, until I realize I'm not hungry after all.

It's 11:57 when my mom walks into my room. I know this from the digital clock on my windowsill.

"Josie?" she says—whispering, in case I'm asleep.

I'm tempted to say, "About time." But I don't. I just make my breath go deep and even, then wait to see what she does next.

She leaves. That's what she does.

After she's gone, I lie there in the dark, wide awake. I think about how she used to come into my room in the middle of the night, when she couldn't sleep, and she'd wake me up. "Do you want to come in my bed?" she'd ask.

And I'd say, "No, thanks, Mommy."

"OK," she'd say.

And then I'd say, "Do *you* want to come in *my* bed?"

And she would, every time. She'd slide under the covers next to me, and we'd talk—or, more accurately, *she'd* talk, and I'd drift off to sleep again, smelling her balsam shampoo and feeling the cool smoothness of her palm against my forehead, brushing back my hair.

I don't know why I'm thinking about this now. She hasn't done it for years. And *believe me*, I wouldn't want her to start up again. It's just weird that she didn't even try to wake me. Not even to talk. Not even to tell me she was home.

✳ ✳ ✳

I wake up to nothing. No pounding of my mom's running shoes on the stairs. No banging of pans in the kitchen. I peek into her bedroom and there she is, a lump under the covers. Which is what a person gets for staying out all night.

I clear my throat, and she mumbles something, but she doesn't wake up.

So I go downstairs to the kitchen and pour myself a bowl of cornflakes because, even though I'm not hungry, it's a game day, and on game days, Coach makes us promise to eat breakfast.

Coach is big on "carbo-loading." He's also big on telling us that, on game days, we are "representing" EHS, which means we're supposed to look "presentable." No jeans, no sweats, no sneakers. Some girls on our team use game days as an opportunity to break school records. This morning it's Schuyler (tightest dress); Jamie (shortest skirt); and Liv (most liberal interpretation of the word "presentable"). Here is what she's wearing: one of those faux tuxedo T-shirts complete with corsage, black velour pants, patent leather Mary Janes with three-inch heels, and—I kid you not—a maroon velvet top hat.

"Wow," I said, when she first stepped onto the bus. "Willy Wonka goes to the prom?"

Liv laughed. "Something like that."

Now, walking down the junior corridor, she's getting all sorts of looks—the kind of looks your average person would die of embarrassment to be getting.

Liv doesn't notice—she's mastered the art of walking and texting—and even if she did notice, she wouldn't care.

Now I'm at my locker, going through my assignment book, making sure I have everything. English essay? *Check.* . . . Trig homework? *Check.* . . . Finger, tapping my shoulder? . . .

Finger, tapping my shoulder.

I turn, and there he is. *Here* he is.

"Hey," Matt Rigby says, smiling. "Game today?"

"Yeah," I say. I'm wearing a denim skirt, shortish, and a red sweater, tightish. Not too revealing, but not too boring, either.

"You look . . . really nice." I notice his eyes linger just a moment on my chest before he lifts his head and blushes.

"Well . . ." I say. "You do too." He's wearing the standard guy's game-day uniform: oxford shirt, khakis, loafers. His sleeves are rolled up. The hairs on his arms are golden.

"Are you home or away?" he asks.

"Home. East Longmeadow. You?"

"Away. Chicopee."

I nod. "Chicopee's tough."

"Yeah. . . . So, I was wondering if I could have your number?" He reaches into his shirt pocket and takes out his cell. "That way we can . . . you know . . . talk after our games."

"OK," I say. No doubt my face is the color of my sweater.

"Cool."

"Let me just get your number too," I say, reaching

casually into my backpack to pull out my cell, like this kind of thing happens every day.

My mom comes to my game like she always does, but she brings Jonathan with her. There they are, snuggled up together on the bleachers under some plaid blanket, with their matching Dunkin' Donuts cups. I try to do what Missy Travers used to tell us: "Keep your head in the game." But that's easier said than done, even when I'm harsh about it. *Keep your goddamn head in the game, Josie.* We're down 1–0 and I've missed three shots already.

There are so many things I want to say to my mother right now.

"I suck today," I tell Liv, who's playing center-half and keeps passing to me. "Schuy's wide open on the right, though. Dump it to her."

"You sure?" she says.

"We need to score."

Liv nods. "Let's do this thing."

My mom hugs me afterward. Even though I played like crap, we won, 3–2. "Way to go," Jonathan says, clomping me on the shoulder. His sandy hair is blowing sideways in the wind. His nose is red at the tip. "Great game."

"Uh-huh," I say. What I really want to say is, *Why are you here? Don't you have violins to tune or something?*

I turn to my mom. "We should go. I have a trig test tomorrow."

My mom turns to Jonathan. As if she needs to *check with him*. I want to grab her hand and yank, the way I would when I was five and we were standing in a torturously long line at the post office.

"I *really* have to study," I add, for emphasis.

You would think that Jonathan would take the hint, but he doesn't. "I was horrible at trig," he says. He crinkles his eyes at me. "I guess that's why I became a music teacher instead of a math teacher."

I nod. As if I care.

"Do you play any instruments, Josie?" Jonathan asks. His head is cocked to one side, like a parrot's. A sandy-haired, red-nosed parrot.

I start to say no, but my mom pipes in, "You play the recorder." Then, to Jonathan, "Josie plays the recorder."

"I don't play—"

"The recorder!" Jonathan's face lights up. "That's great! If you can play the recorder, the clarinet is just—"

"I do not *play the recorder*. I played it for a *week*, in third grade. And I hated it." I shoot my mother a look, as in, *What the hell?*

She smiles. "Miss Mundt said you showed a lot of promise." To Jonathan, "Miss Mundt was Josie's third-grade teacher."

Instead of sharing in the maternal pride-fest, I am

annoyed—mad, in fact, that my mother is using me as a way to flirt with Jonathan. *Listen to these cute little factoids about Josie from when she was a child.* And even though my mother is the one I'm mad at, I turn to Jonathan and say, "I'm not a band geek, if that's what you're asking. . . . I'm more into sports, you know?"

Yes. He's turning red.

My mother stares at me, surprised. Hurt.

I stare right back at her, say nothing.

Jonathan, finally taking the hint, says he has to go. He gives my mom a peck on the cheek and hightails it across the parking lot.

"You were rude," my mother says when we get to our car.

"Excuse me?" I say.

"To Jonathan, back there. You were very rude."

I turn to her. "Are you serious?"

"I would never act that way with one of your friends," she says, and her voice is tight. "Never."

"Oh, he's your *friend* now?"

"You're missing the point."

"No, I'm not."

"We were talking about your manners."

"No, we weren't. *You* were talking about my manners. And if you want to talk about manners, let's talk about the fact that you invited someone to my game without my permission."

"What?"

"I played like crap! Did you even notice? Or were you too busy playing footsie under the blanket?"

She turns to look me straight in the eye. "Is that really what you think?"

I shrug.

Now she turns away, silent, staring out the window. After a minute, "You know something, Josie? Not every-thing is about you."

"Oh," I say, nodding. "OK. So, what—everything's about you now? Is that it?"

"I didn't *say* that." She sounds angry. At me. *I* am the reason for her anger.

"Well," I say, "why don't you try saying what you mean?"

She sighs. "What I *mean* . . . Josie, what I mean is I need to have a life too. Outside of being your mom. I don't want to be just a mom for the rest of my life. OK?"

I hold very still.

"Josie." She actually has the nerve to put her hand on my arm. "Jonathan is important to me. Do you understand what I'm saying?"

I nod slowly. I am trying not to let the volcano that's erupting between my ears spew out of my mouth.

"Good." She turns the key in the ignition, presses the gas.

We drive about three yards.

"By the way," I say casually, like I'm about to mention some fun but inconsequential fact, like the soccer team getting new jerseys. "Paul Tucci's dad came into the café last night."

My mother puts on the brakes and turns to me, stunned. "What?"

I shrug. "Actually, he's been in a few times. I guess they're back in the area. . . . I would have mentioned it sooner, but I didn't think it was a big deal. . . ."

Liar, liar, pants on fire.

"Right," she mumbles, nodding. "No, you're right. It's . . . not a big deal."

But I can see her face—the truth, smeared all over it.

Was it a mistake, telling her? Am I supposed to feel bad now? This is what I'm asking myself on the ride home, which is dead silent, like a hearse full of guilt.

But then I think, *No.*

They did move back here. Big Nick did come into the store. These are the facts. And if my mother can't handle it, that's her problem. It's not my job to tiptoe around her. She's thirty-three years old. She's an *adult.*

My mom pulls into the driveway, and we both get out. We say nothing to each other on our way to the house, or after we get inside. We just walk upstairs to our separate bedrooms and shut our separate doors.

I sit at my desk for a long time, trying to study. After a fruitless hour or so, my cell phone rings. My stomach jumps. I let it ring once, twice, part of a third time before I answer. "Hello?"

"Josie?"

"Yeah?" I say, like I can't quite place the voice.

"It's, uh, Matt. . . . Rigby."

"Oh," I say. "Hey."

"Hey. What are you doing?"

"Nothing. Studying."

"Oh. Do you want to go?"

"Definitely *not*," I say.

And he laughs. It's the best sound I've heard all day.

"How was your game?" he asks.

"We won. Three-two. You guys?"

"Us too. One-zip."

"Nice."

"Yeah. It came down to penalty kicks. Pretty intense."

"I love those kind of games."

"Yeah. Me too." There's a pause. Then he says, "So . . ."

"So . . ."

"So, what else about your day?"

"What else about my *day*?"

"Yeah. Tell me something about the great Josie Gardner."

"Like what?"

"I don't know. Something deep and revealing . . . like . . . what did you have for lunch?"

I smile. "PB and J."

"A classic. White or wheat?"

"Neither. English muffin."

"Real-ly."

"Yup."

"Interesting. OK. . . . Something that made you laugh."

"Liv's outfit."

"Right. The top hat. Very nice. . . . Something that pissed you off."

"Seriously?"

"Yeah."

I hesitate, then say, "My mother."

"Your mother," he repeats.

"Yeah. It's . . . kind of a long story."

"Well," he says. "I've got time."

"Yeah?"

"Tell me. . . . I mean, if you want."

"I don't know. . . ."

"That's cool. No pressure."

"OK," I say.

And then I spill.

Nine

SOMETIMES, NOT OFTEN, a miracle occurs. Like every morning for the past week, Riggs has been waiting at my locker. *How is this happening?* I ask myself each time I see him. There must be some mistake—some glitch in the system. Maybe Cupid got drunk and shot the wrong two people with his arrow. One of these days he'll show up in the cafeteria with his wings askew and brandy on his breath, saying, "Oops! Sorry about that," and snap us out of it.

So far that hasn't happened. So far, things have been . . . well . . . very cool. We talk on the phone almost every night. Not just chat, but really talk. About real things, like my mother, who continues to act like someone I don't know; and Jazzy Jonathan, who continues to bug me; and Matt's parents' divorce; and his psycho stepsister; and the fact that

Paul Tucci's father *keeps showing up* at Fiorello's. Not that my mother would know. Because she hasn't asked. Because ever since I told her about the Tuccis moving back, she has been completely mute on the subject. So I haven't said a word. Don't ask, don't tell.

"I have to meet him," Liv announces one day after practice. "The famous Big Nick. It's time."

"No, it's not," I say.

"Yes, it is. When are you working tonight?"

"Six to nine."

"You have wireless, right?"

"Yeah, but—"

"Good. I'll bring my laptop."

"Please don't come," I say, even though I know it's pointless. You can't tell Liv not to do something, because she'll just laugh and do it anyway. Take College Boy Finn and this booty-call arrangement they have going. A few days ago I raised my concerns—you know, as a friend—and what did Liv do? She laughed. She laughed and dismissed it with a flick of her wrist. "He's not using me, Jose. It's mutual. We're using *each other*."

Well, what do I know? The furthest Riggs and I have gone is second base, in the backseat of his car. (Listen to me, still using the base system, like I'm twelve.) But truthfully, I'm glad we're taking it slow.

Slow is good.

Slow keeps a person's head on straight, which is exactly what I need to do where Riggs is concerned: hold on to my head.

"Wow," Liv says. "This place looks amazing."

It's her first time in Fiorello's. She's lounging on one of the fluffiest chairs, feet propped up on an ottoman, and I have brought her my specialty: the Joseaccino, which is basically a cappuccino with every conceivable topping, including cookie crumbs.

"It does look good, doesn't it?" I say, glancing around, feeling pride in everything Bob has accomplished. The glass tables are so clean you can see yourself, and the air smells sweet and buttery. Piano music wafts out of the speakers on the ceiling—the opposite of that Top-40 crap they play at the Pizza Palace, or any of the other places people our age hang out.

"So," Liv says, placing her mug on a coaster and lowering her voice. "Where is he?"

"How should I know?" I say.

It's not like Big Nick comes in every day. More like every three. He does have a routine, though, when he arrives. He walks right up to the counter and says hello, always with a smile and a wink, like the two of us share a secret. Which is pretty ironic, when you think about it. Sometimes a question will bubble up my throat and into my mouth: *So, how's your son Paul?* But I make myself swallow it, say, "What can I get you tonight?"

Then he'll ask which pastries are good, and I'll tell him. He always orders the same amount: three if they're big; six if they're mini. Plus a hot cocoa. And he always sits at the same table—the little round one in the back, next to the trio of ferns—and he works on the *New York Times* crossword puzzle. He wears glasses when he does this. They're slightly dorky, black and horn-rimmed, and they slide down his nose. He keeps them in the breast pocket of his shirt, the same place he keeps his pen.

Don't ask me why I've noticed these things.

"Well," Liv says. "I might as well do some homework while I'm waiting."

"You do that," I say.

She pulls out her laptop.

I go back behind the counter, not because there are customers, but because I need to be doing something. Something mindless, like . . . filling the sugar shakers. Yes. This is what I will do. I will collect all the sugar shakers, and I will fill them.

Done.

I ask Bob for another task, and he hands me a bucket of cookie dough. Could I ball the dough and put it on trays to bake at 350? Yes, I could. I could also make the chai tea and scrub down the coffeemaker and replace the hot-drink lids at the milk station. Anyone watching me would say, *Wow, what a little worker bee. Does she ever stop?*

And the answer would be yes. I stop every time the front door tinkles. I stop, and I look, and then, once I see who it is, I breathe.

Lady in red hat. *Phew.*

Man in Patriots jersey. *Phew.*

Couple in matching earmuffs. *Phew.*

I take orders, smile, make drinks. Think: *He's not coming in tonight, pressure's off, good.* Liv can't pull one of her crazy moves. I know what she's capable of. I once listened to her argue with my English teacher for fifteen minutes about the B-minus he gave me on a paper about *Tom Sawyer.* I have also spent an entire afternoon with her in a store called Womanly Pleasures, where she made the saleslady describe for me, in graphic detail, the virtues of various vibrators.

This is what I'm up against.

I grab a sponge, because Liv is such a slob she can't drink without spilling. I will sponge down her table. Also, tell her she's welcome to leave now.

"Finish your homework?" I say.

"Oh. Yeah." Liv looks up from her laptop, yawns. "You should see Finn's MyPage. He pasted, like, a million album covers together, all different colors, to form this mosaic of Bob Marley's face. Check it out. . . ."

I check it out. Not that I don't already have the picture.

Mr. Uber-Cool, Funky-Retro-College Dude. Mr. Sideburns and John Lennon Glasses. Mr. I-Sleep-with-Sixteen-Year-Old-High-School-Babes, Aren't-I-Rad? I still don't get what Liv is doing with him, but at least *she* seems to know.

"Cool, huh?" Liv says, still gazing at the mosaic thingy.

"Uh-huh," I say. I go to work, sponging her table.

"He's going away this weekend. Some concert. . . . I guess I won't see him until—"

Tinkle, tinkle, tinkle.

"—next week, which is—"

I freeze, midsponge . . .

"—such a bummer."

And the door swings open.

"Josie?"

I turn to Liv, look her hard in the eyes, and say nothing.

Liv glances at the door, then back at me. She raises her eyebrows.

I nod.

Liv and I have been friends for so long, we've developed our own telepathic shorthand.

"Go," she whispers. "Take his order."

"I will," I say. Then, I hold up a finger of warning. "Not a word. You understand? Not a *peep*."

Liv gives me her Mona Lisa smile.

"I mean it," I tell her.

My instinct, based on years of experience, is to shove her out the door onto the street. That's the only guarantee that she will mind her own business. But then she'd probably just come back another night.

I can't win. So I walk over to the counter.

Big Nick is wearing a scarf, red and black, the homemade variety, and I wonder briefly if Mrs. Tucci knit it for him.

"Evening, Josie." Smile, wink. "What's good tonight?"

"These," I say, pointing to the top tray of cookies. "I just took them out of the oven."

"Ahh," he says, rubbing his hands together. "Great. I'll take half a dozen."

Bob swoops up behind me with a bakery box and starts loading cookies into it. I turn around to make the cocoa.

This is my tragic mistake: turning around. With my back to Liv, I can't see her coming.

"Hi, there. . . ."

But I can hear her.

"Olivia Weiss-Longo. I'm Josie's best friend."

I whip back around to see them shaking hands.

"Nico Tucci. . . . Big Nick."

"*Big Nick*. I like it."

My death stare is no match for Liv's charming smile. By the time I hand Big Nick his mug, he's a goner—completely under her spell.

Later, I am lying on the pullout couch in the Weiss-Longos' den, which Dodd has made up for me. The mattress is lumpy with a metal bar underneath that digs into the middle of your back all night. Liv is sitting next to me, giving me puppy-dog eyes.

"You're a piece of work," I say.

Her mouth forms a tiny "O" of innocence.

"I can't believe you sat with him. I can't believe you even *talked* to him!"

"Well, I couldn't very well *sit* with him and not make *conversation*," she says, one hand on her chest. "That would be rude."

I don't know what to say, so I grab a pillow and whack her in the head. Once, twice, half of a third time before she rips it out of my hands. "OK, OK! . . . I deserve to be beaten."

"Yes," I tell her. "You do."

"I know." She nods solemnly. Then she picks up the pillow and smacks herself in the face, hard. "Bad Liv."

I start to smile, then stop myself. "No. You are not getting off the hook this time."

"OK."

"I'm mad at you."

"I know."

"Because you deliberately ignored my request—"

"Yes."

"Showing no regard whatsoever for my feelings."

"Right," Liv says, nodding. Then, "No! I didn't 'show no regard for your feelings.' You're the one I did it for."

"Oh my God!" I laugh-snort, feeling a tiny spark of

anger flicker in my chest. "You're so . . . do you really think I need you to *do* things for me? Do you not think I can make decisions on my *own*? I mean . . . come on, Liv! It's insulting!"

"OK." Her cheeks are pink suddenly, like she gets it.

"You know?"

"Yes. I'm sorry."

"OK, then," I say. "Good."

She's quiet for a second, reaching down to play with a tassel on the edge of the blanket.

"So . . ." I say.

She looks up. "So?"

"So, what did you talk about?"

She shrugs. "Oh, things."

"What things?"

"Just things. About your dad and your grandmother and stuff. . . . You wouldn't be interested."

"*Liv.*"

"What? You said you didn't want anything to do with them. . . ."

I grab the pillow, hold it over her head.

"OK!" She's smiling now. She scoots her body in closer, places both hands on her knees, leans in. "OK, so Mrs. Tucci? Christina? She doesn't let him have any sugar, so—"

"I know." From that night at Shop-Co, the Peppermint Pattie exchange. "*I* told *you* that."

Liv heaves a sigh. "Do you want me to keep going, Josie? Or not. Because it's no skin off my nose—"

"Yes," I say. "Go."

"So he tells her he's going bowling."

"What?"

Liv laughs. "Yeah! He used to be in this bowling league, back in Arizona? So that's what he tells her he's doing, whenever he comes to Fiorello's. . . . Bowling at Elmherst Lanes."

"Great," I say. "So he's a liar."

"He's not a *liar.*"

I give her a look.

"OK, so he tells his wife a little fib so he can have a cookie or two. Is that so bad? I tell Pops and Dodd I'm going to the library when I'm really going to see Finn, and you don't call *me* a liar."

I shrug. "That's different."

"How? How is that different?"

"I don't know. It just is. Just . . . keep going. What about . . . you know . . . ?"

"Your dad?"

I shake my head. *"Paul."*

Liv nods. "OK, *Paul. Paul* is living in North Carolina. Raleigh. He runs one of those outdoor-ed programs for . . . you know, troubled youth. With, like, climbing walls and zip lines and stuff."

"Really?"

"Uh-huh. His older brothers are down there too. The Outer Banks, though, where they spent all their summers. Big Nick and Christina still have their beach house, so they visit all the time. . . . Patrick's the oldest, a pilot, and . . . another 'P' name. . . . *Peter*, I think . . . does . . . something financial. Investment banking?"

"Huh," I say.

"Yeah," Liv says. Then, "Think about it, Jose. You have *uncles*."

"Well . . ."

"And *cousins*."

"I have cousins?"

She nods. "Three. Big Nick whipped out the wallet photos. The moms are really pretty, in a Southern belle-ish sort of way. You know, lots of hair and lipstick—" Liv stops. She must have seen something in my face because her hand moves gently to my arm. "Do you want me to shut up?"

"I don't know." My voice sounds small.

"It's a lot to take in."

I nod.

"That grandfather of yours is a real chatterbox."

I nod again. It's all I can do.

Liv is silent for a moment, and so am I. But the question I need to ask is swelling in my chest, too big to hold in. "Does he . . . Paul . . . have kids?"

Liv looks at me, smiles.

Oh, God. He does.

"Yeah. A sixteen-year-old daughter named Josie."

"Oh." I feel myself sigh a little.

"Jose?"

"Yeah," I say.

"He's not even married."

"What?"

"He has a girlfriend. But he's not married."

"Oh," I say.

There is so much in my head right now. I need to lie down, cover my face with a pillow, let it all soak in.

Later, Pops comes into the den, where Liv and I are sprawled on the pullout couch in our pajamas. "It's Kate," he says, holding out the cordless phone to me. I have no choice but to take it.

"What's up?" I say as Pops walks out, clicking the door shut behind him.

"What's *up*?" There's an edge to my mother's voice. "Why aren't you answering your cell?"

"I didn't hear it ring," I tell her, which isn't a lie. The battery's dead and my charger's at home.

"Well, when exactly were you planning on calling me? I had no idea where you were."

"I left a note," I say, keeping my tone cool.

"Where?"

"Right there, on the kitchen counter. Next to the fruit bowl."

There's a pause. The sound of footsteps. Then she says, "Well . . . you still should have called."

"Right. The way you *always* call when you're out with Jonathan, to let me know *exactly* when you'll be coming home."

If this were a sarcasm contest, I'd be kicking ass.

"This isn't about Jonathan. This is about you and me, and the fact that I am still your mother, and because I am your mother, I need to know where you are."

"Right," I say. "As I indicated. With the note."

"Besides which," she continues, like she hasn't heard a word I've said, "it's a school night. And I don't think you should be having sleepovers on school nights. You need your rest."

I love how she's trying to sound all parental right now. How many school nights have I spent sitting next to her on the couch, watching *90210* until midnight?

"Is Jonathan there?" I ask.

"No. He just dropped me off."

Of course he did, I want to say. *Because you can't go a single day without seeing him, can you?*

But I don't. What I do is mutter good-bye and toss the phone onto a chair beside the couch.

Liv raises her eyebrows. "What was *that*?"

"What?"

"I've never heard you talk to Kate like that."

I shrug.

"You sounded like *Mel*."

"Yeah, well. My mom is starting to sound a lot like Mrs. Jaffin."

Liv doesn't say anything, just shakes her head and starts playing with some fringe on the edge of a pillow.

"What," I say.

"Nothing."

"You obviously have something to say, so say it."

Liv turns to me, and her eyes are serious. She tells me I don't know how lucky I am to have Kate. She says that she wouldn't trade Pops and Dodd for anything, but it's not the same. It's not like having a mom to talk to.

"Well . . . you *have* a mom, technically."

Liv shoots me a look.

"What? You do."

"An egg donor surrogate is not a *mom*. She's an *incubator*."

"Not *just* an incubator," I say. "She sends Christmas cards."

It's true. Every year, Liv and Wyatt's egg-donor surrogate sends a Christmas card from Minnesota, wishing the Weiss-Longos a warm and wonderful new year. I am tempted to point out that Paul Tucci has never sent *me* a Christmas card, but I decide to keep this to myself. Because Liv is frowning.

"You're right, Josie. Those Christmas cards are just like a *real mom*! Just *chock-full* of maternal wisdom and comfort. . . . I feel such a *kindred connection* to the annual Hallmark greeting that represents the *random woman* Pops and Dodd *paid* to lug me around in her womb for nine months—"

"OK, OK," I say.

But Liv isn't finished. "We're so close, me and my egg-donor surrogate, we communicate telepathically!"

I wince and tell her I'm sorry. Because I am. I never should have brought it up.

She sighs. "Whatever. You're completely missing my point. Do you want to hear it, or not?"

I don't, but I nod anyway.

"You shouldn't take Kate for granted, Josie. She's a great mom. The more you fight with her—"

"We're not *fighting*."

"OK, the worse you treat her—"

"*Me?*" I say. "There were two sides to that conversation, Liv. You only heard one."

She shakes her head. "Regardless, you *still* have a choice about how you act."

I stare at her, feeling my face heat up. "And this is your business because . . ."

"I'm your best friend."

"You could have fooled me," I say, surprised at the

hardness in my voice. "You always take my mom's side, you know that? . . . You think she can do no wrong. Well, let me tell you something: She can."

"It's not about taking *sides*, Josie. I love you both." Liv reaches over, touching my arm with her hand.

I shake it off. "Whatever." Then, sounding like a ten-year-old girl on the playground, I say, "I thought best friends meant total loyalty."

"It *does*," Liv says. "I *am*."

I don't respond. We sit in silence for a while. Then, she says, "Are you still pissed?"

"Yes," I say.

"Would you feel better if you smacked me upside the head?"

"Yes," I say again. I can feel myself start to smile but fight it. "Smack upside the head" is one of Liv's and my favorite expressions. Ever since second grade, when Timmy O'Keefe threatened to smack our gym teacher, Mr. Lyons, upside the head, for telling him he threw like a girl.

"Go on, then," Liv says, leaning in closer. "Smack me. Right upside the head. And after that, I'll smack *you* upside the head."

I smirk, bite my lip, smirk again.

And then, of course, I crack up.

Ten

IN THE MORNING, when I get out of the shower, Liv is sitting at her desk in her pajamas, staring at the computer.

"What are you doing?" I ask.

She shrugs.

I lean in to look.

"Pregnant Teen Help dot org?"

She nods.

I swallow. "Please tell me you're researching something for school . . . some health project, or . . ."

Silence.

"Liv."

More silence.

"Oh my God, are you serious?"

She shakes her head. "I don't know."

"You think you're . . ."

"I don't know. Maybe. I just yakked." She points to the trash can. "I couldn't even make it to the bathroom."

"Well," I say briskly, "you probably just have that stomach bug. The one Schuyler had. She was out all last week."

"Did Schuyler's boobs hurt?"

"Your *boobs* hurt?"

"I don't know."

"Well, do they or don't they?"

She shakes her head again. "Maybe. A little. Maybe I'm just being paranoid. But my period's late. I know that."

"*How* late?"

"Three days."

I breathe out. "Well," I say. I grab the other desk chair, sit down next to her. "Three days is nothing."

"You think?" she says, looking at me with eyes that are suddenly too big for her face.

"Listen to me," I say. "I've been three days late before. I've been a whole *week* late. It doesn't necessarily mean anything."

"Well, not if you're a *virgin*."

"Well, yeah. Obviously. But even if you're not a virgin. . . . Wait. You and Finn *have* been using protection, right?"

"Of course."

"Every time?"

Liv gives me a look. "Josie, do you think I'm an idiot?"

"No. No, of course I don't. Just . . . Liv, you cannot freak out over three days. You'll drive yourself crazy."

"I know. I am."

"It could be stress, hormones, diet. . . . All sorts of things can affect your cycle."

"I know."

I hesitate, then ask, "Do you want to take a . . . you know . . . test?"

She shakes her head. "Not yet. I don't want to know yet. I just want to . . . not know for a few more days."

"OK, so we'll wait, then. And stay calm."

"Right." Liv nods. "OK. You do the calm part, though, because I don't know if I can."

"I will," I tell her.

"Thanks."

We hug. I hold on tight, too, because something just dawned on me. *This* is where Liv was coming from last night. *This* is why she went off on me. Her whole "you're so lucky to have Kate, you shouldn't take Kate for granted" spiel now makes perfect sense. Liv really needs a real mom to talk to. Not just an egg-donor surrogate from Minnesota who doesn't know squat.

All day, I try to make her laugh. "Hey, Liv," I say as we're changing for gym, "I have a joke for you. Knock-knock."

"Josie. I'm really not in the mood."

"Come on," I say. "Knock-knock."

She heaves a sigh. "Who's there?"

"Norma Lee."

"Norma Lee who?"

"Normalee I don't go around knocking on doors, but would you like to buy a set of encyclopedias?"

Liv doesn't exactly laugh, but her lips twitch a little, which is good enough for me.

When we're on the bus to our game against Palmer Regional, I try again. "So there are these two muffins in the oven, right?"

"If you say so," Liv says.

"They're both sitting there, just chilling and getting baked. After a while, one muffin yells, 'God damn, it's hot in here!' and the other muffin replies, 'Holy crap, a talking muffin!'"

"I'm surprised at you, Josephine," Liv says dryly. "Druggie humor."

"*Baking* humor," I say. "And anyway, don't blame me. Blame Big Nick. He's the one who told it to me."

"Ah." She nods. "You've been bonding."

"We have not been *bonding*."

"It sounds like you've been bonding."

"Let's get one thing straight, OK? Big Nick is a customer. And I'm just serving up pastries and laughing at his jokes like I would with anyone else. That is all. But if you feel the need to read something Dr. Steveian into every little interaction, you go right ahead. . . ."

"Wow, are you defensive."

"I am not defensive! I'm just trying to act normal around the guy! OK? Can you let me do that?"

"OK," Liv says. "I won't bring it up again."

"Yes, you will."

Now Kara and Lindsey are leaning over the back of our seat, wanting to talk about the game. We discuss strategy. We tell each other how awesome we've been playing lately. We agree there's no way we're losing today.

Ten minutes later, we're pulling into the Palmer Regional parking lot.

"Ready to kick some ass?" I ask Liv.

She nods.

"What's that? I didn't hear you. . . . I said, *Are you ready to—*"

"Josie?" Her voice is barely audible.

"What?" I notice how pale her face is. Pale and pinched. "Liv . . ."

She closes her eyes.

"Are you going to—"

She nods, grabs her duffel bag, and barfs into it.

"It's OK," I tell her. "You're OK."

I rub her back and say a silent prayer, to whatever celestial being might be listening right now. *Please. Please let this be a stomach bug.*

Eleven

THE NEXT MORNING, in front of my locker, Matt Rigby kisses me sweet and slow. Then he pulls back and grins.

"What's that for?" I ask.

"Your hat trick." He means the three goals I scored yesterday while Liv was on the bench, turning various shades of green. "Congrats."

"Thanks," I say, even though we already had this conversation last night on the phone. It's way better having it in person.

"My parents want to meet you," he says.

"Because of the hat trick?"

"Because I won't shut up about you. . . . Next Saturday, after our games. Can you come for dinner? Becky's making lasagna."

Becky, the stepmother. Matt's real mom, Darlene, split from his dad when Matt was a baby and moved to some hippie colony in Vermont. Matt only sees her a few times a year. Becky pretty much raised him.

"Lasagna," I say. "Yum."

"Yeah. Becky's a great cook. . . . My dad, he's kind of old-school about . . . you know . . . meeting the people I hang out with."

"The people you hang out with. . . . And just how many people are you hanging out with, currently?"

He leans in, kisses the tip of my nose. "Just one."

"You sure about that?"

Another kiss. This time on the lips. "Absolutely."

"Good."

"So you'll come?" he says, kissing me again, softly, on the side of my neck, just below my left ear.

"Yes." I have goose bumps now, running all the way down the left side of my body. "I will."

I was planning to tell my mom about dinner at the Rigbys'. I was also planning to tell her about Liv, to ask her advice. But both of those plans just got derailed.

"Jonathan has tickets for the B.B. King Jazz Festival," she tells me as we're driving home from work. "This weekend, in Portsmouth, New Hampshire. He asked me to go with him."

"Wow," I say. "You've really embraced the jazz."

She ignores my sarcasm. "I told him I needed to check with you, before I said yes. It would only be the one night. We'd leave Saturday morning."

"You don't need to *check with me*. You're the adult."

"I'm trying to be respectful of your feelings, Josie. OK? I'm trying to do this right."

"Right," I say. "You and Jonathan want my blessing to go away for the weekend? Fine. Consider yourselves blessed."

"I really appreciate the smart-ass routine, Josie. Thanks."

"Anytime, Kate. Anytime."

Later, I hear her on the phone with Jonathan. Her voice is muffled, but I know she's talking about me. And I hate it. Because she never would have talked behind my back before. She would have done it to my face.

We've forgotten how to talk to each other. And it hurts. More than I would have thought.

Liv stays home from school on Tuesday.

And Wednesday.

On Thursday, she's back on the bus, but she still hasn't gotten her period. And no, she hasn't taken a test. And no, she doesn't want to talk about it. She doesn't even want to *think* about it. My job, therefore, is to distract.

"I'm staying at your house this weekend," I say. "My mom's going to New Hampshire. With Jonathan."

"I know," she says.

"How?"

"Kate called. She talked to Dodd."

Right.

"So," Liv says. "This Jonathan thing is serious."

I make a noise, like a grunt.

"Are you OK?"

I shrug.

"Well?" Liv says. Her brown eyes are wide and lined with green pencil. "Are you, or aren't you?"

"I don't know," I say. "No."

"Have you talked to Kate about it?"

"No."

"Josie. Come on. You have to talk to her."

"I can't," I say.

"Why not?"

"Have you talked to Pops and Dodd about your 'situation'?"

"No, but that's—"

"See?"

"But—"

"No buts," I say. "I'm not talking to her."

"Fine," Liv says. "Tell me, then. I'm curious. What's wrong with Jonathan?"

"I don't *know.*"

"Bad breath?"

"No."

"Verbal abuse?"

"No."

"Does he pick his nose and wipe it on his pants?"

"*No.* It's . . . OK. Here's what it is. I look at the two of them together and . . . I don't see it. You know? I don't *get it.* I don't feel the love connection. I've tried. But it's just not there."

"Maybe you don't *want* to see it," Liv says.

"What's that supposed to mean?"

"Maybe, deep down, you don't actually want Kate to have someone. No matter how great he is."

"Of course I want her to have someone! I just want him to be . . ."

"What," Liv says.

"I don't know."

"Paul Tucci?"

"*What?*" I stare at her.

"You heard me."

"Are you high?"

"No."

"You think I want my mom and Paul Tucci to get back together."

"Maybe. Yeah."

"Well. That's ridiculous."

Liv shakes her head. "I don't mean consciously."

"Oh," I say. "Uh-huh."

"It's your subconscious desire."

"Right."

"It is. You just can't see it because it's buried."

"Whatever, Dr. Steve," I say. And I say "whatever" a bunch more times too as we're getting off the bus.

Twelve

"DO YOU WANT a ride?" my mother asks.

It's Saturday morning and we're standing in the driveway, watching Jonathan unload and reload the trunk of his car. Because the two of them are off on their New Hampshire adventure—their jazzy little jaunt. In a way, I'm glad they're going. Now I won't have to think about them for thirty-six hours.

"Do you want us to drop you off?" my mom asks again.

"No, thanks," I say.

"Fiorello's is on our way. We'd be happy to."

"That's OK."

"I'm sure Jonathan would let you drive, if you want. You could get in a little practice. . . ."

Since I got my permit, my mom has barely taken me driving at all. She gets too nervous. It kills me to say no right now, but I do. I tell her I'll take the bus.

"Why would you take the bus when you come with us?"

"Mom! God! Why are you pushing me to go with you?"

She sighs, exasperated. Then her face softens slightly and she says, "Why do we keep fighting?"

"I don't know," I say, which is half true. When she looks at me, I shrug. "What do you want me to say?"

She shakes her head. "I just . . . hate this."

"Yeah," I tell her. "Me too."

After they leave, I am upstairs packing because I have to go to my game from work, and Riggs's house from my game. There's a shirt of my mom's I want to borrow, this black scoop neck, so I go in her room to look for it.

The place is a mess. Clothes everywhere. It looks like a cyclone hit, but after a lot of digging I find the shirt. I sit on the edge of my mom's bed to put it on, and my butt hits something hard. I look under the covers, and what do I find? The yearbook.

The yearbook.

I pick it up, of course. I pick it up and I flip to page 102, which is dog-eared for instant access. I stare at Paul Tucci's senior portrait, shake my head. Think: *My mother is still sleeping with my father.*

Five thirty-five p.m. I am riding shotgun in the Riggsmobile, which smells like cleats and French fries. We are on our way to Casa Rigby, to eat Becky's lasagna.

There's no reason to be nervous, is what my head is saying. It's just dinner. They're just people.

But no. I am not convincing myself.

Riggs is steering with one hand, twining my fingers with the other. When he asks for the play-by-play of my game, I tell him that we won four to three. I scored one goal (corner kick), Schuyler scored one goal (penalty), and Liv scored two (both headers). I leave out the fact that thirteen minutes into the second half, Liv called a time-out to use the Porta-John. And that once she got inside, the whole team could hear her yelling for a tampon. And that after I ran over to give her one, we hugged, jumping up and down behind the Porta-John, whooping quietly for joy.

"So," Matt says now, squeezing my hand. "Are you ready for this?"

"Yes," I say. Even though I know his family is going to compare me to Missy Travers. Missy Travers, Blonde Bombshell. Missy Travers, Merit Scholar.

We slow down, turn into the driveway of 7 Geneseo Lane. Matt runs around the car to open the passenger door.

"I thought chivalry was dead," I say.

"Nope." He holds out his hand.

"I'm nervous," I blurt.

He pulls me to my feet and kisses me, right there in his parents' driveway. Sweet and slow. "Better?"

"Uh-huh."

"Good," he says, pulling me toward the house. "Let's go."

At dinner, Matt sits next to me. Every so often he touches me under the table—foot on foot, hand on knee—and I'm glad he does. His stepsister, Kylie, a moonfaced brunette in a boy-band sweatshirt, doesn't stop staring at me for a second, like I'm some strange new species of bug she's never laid eyes on before. I try to ignore her and focus on the parents.

In response to Becky's questions, I tell everyone that my favorite subject in school is English, the girls' soccer team is five and one, and my mom works in a bookstore. When Becky asks about my father, I keep my answer simple: "He lives in North Carolina. He works with at-risk youth."

Under the table, Matt squeezes my hand. I squeeze back.

Becky—an older, doughier version of Kylie—thinks this is wonderful. "Isn't that wonderful, Hank?" she says to Matt's dad—a balding, mustached version of Matt. "Josie's father works with at-risk youth!"

"Wonderful," Mr. Rigby says dryly. "Used to be an at-risk youth myself."

He proceeds to tell the story of how he and his high-school buddies would drive around their town at night, removing all the pink flamingos and garden gnomes and Mary-on-a-half-shells off people's front lawns, and then replant them on the lawn in front of their principal's house.

"My father the juvie," Riggs says, shaking his head.

Matt's dad claps him on the shoulder. "Takes one to know one."

Then, of course, I have to ask, "Is this a family tradition?"

Matt shrugs, embarrassed.

"Absolutely!" Mr. Rigby booms.

"OK," Matt says to me. "I *have* been known to replant the occasional garden gnome. . . ." But then he immediately changes the subject back to soccer.

I can tell he doesn't want me to think badly of him, but in a way, picturing him sneaking around in the middle of the night with his friends, rearranging lawn ornaments, only makes me like him more. It makes me wonder what else I don't know about Matt Rigby.

There's only one embarrassing moment the whole dinner, at the very end, when Matt says he and I are going upstairs and Becky reminds him of the house rule: *Thou shalt not close thy bedroom door.* It makes me wonder how many times Matt brought Missy Travers to his room, and what they did while they were up here.

I am trying not to think about that right now.

Matt and I are collapsed on the oversize foam chair in his room. My stomach is bursting with lasagna. And salad. And garlic bread. And chocolate mousse. "I can't believe how good that was," I say.

"I told you Becky could cook," Matt says, pulling me closer.

"Yeah. . . . They were really nice. And funny. Your dad's high-school stories? I almost peed my pants."

"That's Dad." He smiles, leans in to kiss my cheek. I love it when he smiles. There's this little dimple on the right side of his mouth, every time.

"They made me feel completely comfortable," I babble on. "I mean, completely. It wasn't awkward at all. . . ."

"Good."

"Your dad and Becky seem to have a really good relationship. . . . Like, I *get* now how Darlene could come for Christmas and it wouldn't be weird. . . ." At first when Matt told me about his mother having holidays with his dad and stepmom, it sounded crazy. But now it doesn't. "It's really cool, when you think about it," I say.

"Josie?" Matt says.

"Yeah?"

"Could we stop talking about my family?"

I move my eyes to his eyes, and there is that look, the one Liv always finds so amusing. *Come hither, Hester Prynne.* Heat surges up my neck and onto my cheeks.

"OK," I say.

We kiss.

This is something I could do for hours: kiss Matt Rigby. He has a knack for making every nerve in my body stand at full attention. It starts with my lips, then moves to my tongue, then it slides down and down and down until—

"Wait," I say, pulling back. "What about the door rule?"

"What about it?" Riggs murmurs, pressing his mouth to mine.

We have followed Becky's instructions, but barely. The door to Matt's room is cracked about a centimeter.

"Well . . ." I start to say, "if you think . . ."

But then I shut up. Everything feels too good. Anyway, the door rule is probably just a reminder not to go completely nuts up here; it's not a literal—

"Oh my *God*!" squeals a voice from the doorway. It's Kylie.

Riggs bolts upright, launching his death gaze across the room. "Beat it, Kylie. *Now*."

Kylie shakes her head, sending her ponytail swinging. "*Uh-uhhh*," she singsongs.

"Kylie, I'm warning you . . ." Riggs takes one menacing step toward the door. Then another.

"Mommmmm!" She runs, screaming down the hall. "Mommmmmmm! They're totally going at it up here!"

Riggs turns to me. His cheeks are two flames.

I smile. "There *are* advantages to being an only child."

He shakes his head, swears.

"Hey." I stand up, walk over and wrap both my arms around his waist. "It's OK."

"No, it's not."

I kiss him softly on the chin. "Yes. It is." Then again. "It's fine."

"I just want to be alone with you," he murmurs into my neck. "Just you. And me. And no interruptions."

His breath is hot.

I have goose bumps all over.

I try to suppress the realization that there is a place we could go right now—a place where no one would be. "Let's go for a drive," I suggest. "We can park somewhere and—"

He sighs. "Not the car."

"OK." I take a deep breath, let it out slowly. "My house, then."

"Your house?"

"No one's home. My mom's in New Hampshire, remember?"

Riggs looks at me. "Are you sure?"

"About my mom being in New Hampshire?"

"About going to your house."

I nod, feeling about fifty different ways at once. Nervous. Guilty. Excited. "Yeah," I say. "I'm sure."

He smiles, then crosses the room to open a drawer on his nightstand.

I watch him take something out—something small, silvery—and stuff it into his backpack. My stomach flips over. "Matt?"

"Yeah?"

"That's not . . . you're not . . . I mean, I don't know if I'm ready yet, to . . . you know . . ." I sound like a blathering idiot.

"Josie?" He walks over to me.

"Yeah?"

"It's gum."

"Oh," I say, nodding.

"For our garlic breath."

"Right."

"I have condoms, too. If that's what you're wondering."

"Oh. Uh-huh."

"But that doesn't mean we have to use them. We can just . . . you know . . . hang out, if you want."

"OK," I say, relieved on two levels. A) Matt's smart enough to carry condoms, and B) he's not going to pressure me.

Ten minutes later we are back in his car, driving to my house. In my head—not because I want it to, but because it just pops in there—is a picture of my mom. She is lying on her childhood bed next to Paul Tucci. "So, what do you think, Kate?" he is saying to her, handsome as can be in his North Haven letterman jacket. "Should we go for it?"

Guns N' Roses is playing on the radio.

The *90210* gang watches from the wall.

Everything lies ahead for the two of them. Every possibility. Every opportunity.

Or not.

Depending on her answer.

"So, you guys finally got naked," Liv says.

It's eleven fifteen p.m. and, much to Dodd's relief, we are both home, reclined on the safety of the Weiss-Longo pull-out couch.

"*Partially* naked," I say.

Already I am regretting opening my mouth. What Riggs and I did—or didn't do—belongs to us. It's part of this thing we're growing, this thing that's ours and nobody else's. Whenever I stop to think about it, I can't help myself, this stupid grin starts pulling at my lips and I have to bury my face in a pillow.

I remember in middle school thinking it was all so disgusting. I would *never* touch a guy like that. I would never let *him* do those things to *me*. And now . . . here I am.

"There's a lot more to sex than just intercourse," Liv says, prying the pillow off my face. She looks Boho chic in a velvet beret and tiny paintbrush earrings, in honor of her and Finn's night at the UMass art gallery, hooking up in the darkroom.

"You should know," I say. "You're the sexpert."

"I am not a *sexpert*. I've only had sex with two guys."

She means Avi, the guy from drama camp, and Finn. But there have been other guys she's hooked up with, sans intercourse.

"Relatively speaking," I say, "you're a sexpert."

Liv turns, looks at me. "I have to tell you something."

"What?"

"Finn and I broke up."

"*What?* . . . But tonight . . . the darkroom . . . I thought you guys . . ."

"We didn't, actually. We started to, and then I told him about the period thing, and he dumped me."

"He dumped you *because you got your period*?"

She sighs. "Not exactly. More because it could have gone the other way. I could have *not* gotten it."

"OK, that makes *no* sense."

"He phrased it differently. He said there was too much of an age difference—that I couldn't handle a, quote, *mature sexual partnership*, unquote."

"That's bullshit!"

"I know."

"He's the one who couldn't handle it!"

"I *know*, Josie. It's OK."

"How? How is it OK?"

"It's . . . what Finn and I had was never a partnership at all. We were just . . . hooking up. And even though I love hooking up—I mean, I really *love* it—I've never had . . . like, I look at Pops and Dodd, and I look at you and Riggs, and I'm jealous. I've never had that. *That*, I want."

"Are you serious?"

She nods.

"You put me and Riggs in the same category as Pops and Dodd?"

"Kind of," she says. "Yeah."

I can tell that she means it, and even though I think she's deluded, I say, "You could have that too, if you really want it."

Liv flops back on the bed, sighs. "I don't know."

I start to say, *What about Kevin Kinnear?*—this funky band-geek guy who was madly in love with Liv in middle school, but then I remember her saying, *Kevin Kinnear has a duck face.* Instead, I say, "There are lots of guys who would love to go out with you, if you'd give them a chance."

"You mean high-school guys."

"If you rule out high-school guys, you rule out a lot."

She heaves another sigh. Then she says, "Maybe you're right."

This, coming from the queen of rightness herself. Well. Maybe I will ask Riggs if there's anyone he can think of who'd be a good match for Liv. Someone with a brain. Someone who will appreciate her twisted humor and her flair for fashion. Someone who'll appreciate her worth. I don't know if that person exists at Elmherst High School, but if he does, believe me, I will find him.

Thirteen

SOMETIMES BOB ASKS me to come in on a Sunday early, to do prep work. Today is one of those days. So it's exactly 6:17 a.m., and I am already lining pastry boxes with waxed paper. I am brewing coffee. Picking out a nice Sunday-morning CD—something classical, mellow.

All the while, Bob is scrubbing away. The floor, the chairs, the tabletops. I know he did this last night after closing, yet he is compelled to do it all over again. What does he think went down overnight? A roach wedding? Tiny trolls with wheelbarrows full of E. coli, dumping them everywhere? But you have to give the guy credit; this place is always spotless.

It's 6:57, and someone is knocking on the door. We don't open until eight—it says so right there in black and white—but whoever it is keeps pounding.

"Get that, would you, Josie?" Bob says. He's busy, sliding a pan of sticky buns into the oven.

I yank open the door and there, wearing one of those canvas bucket hats and carrying *The New York Times*, is Big Nick.

"I know you're not open yet," he says. His face looks weird—grayish, with a sort of sheen to it. "But can I come in?" He starts to unzip his fleece jacket.

"Are you OK?" I ask.

"Hot," he says. "Walked too fast."

"OK, um . . ." I turn my head to call Bob, but he's already here, standing at my elbow, rubbing his hands on a paper towel. "Mr. Tucci wants—"

"Our best customer," Bob says, cutting me off. "Come in. Sit." He gestures to the round table in the back.

Big Nick nods. The hat is off now. His hair is sticking up in silver tufts.

"Coffee?" Bob asks.

"Please." Big Nick shuffles over to a chair and sits.

I busy myself straightening the cinnamon and nutmeg shakers on the bar next to his table.

"Can I get you something to eat?" I ask.

He pauses, reaching up to pull his shirt collar away from his throat.

I take a step toward him. "Are you sure you're OK?"

He waves a hand at me. "I'm *fine*." This comes out strong,

like a bark. Then he says, lower, "Sorry. . . . You choose something."

I tell him OK; I'll be right back.

On my way to the counter I wonder briefly if he and Mrs. Tucci had a fight, if that's why he's here so early, acting weird. Maybe she found out he's not really in a bowling league. Maybe he's been lying about other things too, like Mel's dad, who used to say he was working late when really he was shtupping his paralegal, or Schuyler's dad, who drinks. . . . But somehow, I can't imagine Mr. Tucci doing anything like that.

"He wants something to eat," I tell Bob. "What should I—"

"Here," Bob says, handing me a plate. Mini bear claws and chocolate croissants, arranged in the shape of a fan.

"Thanks," I say.

I turn back toward the table. I take about three steps and then, like one of those cheesily dramatic slow-motion movie scenes, I watch, frozen, as Big Nick's head flops to one side and his body slumps over, out of the chair and onto the floor with a sickening thud.

Only this isn't a movie.

This is really happening.

I'm not sure exactly what comes next. I know I drop the plate. I know that Bob murmurs, "Oh my God," and that, for at least a nanosecond, neither of us moves. But then, somehow, Bob is rushing past me, through the scattered pastries and shards of ceramic, and I am stepping back.

He is bending over Big Nick, touching his shoulder and saying his name.

Saying it again.

Saying it again.

Now he is leaning his ear to Big Nick's chest.

I take a step forward. "Is he breathing?"

Bob shakes his head.

"You need to start rescue breaths," I say, walking faster. I know this from our first-aid unit in health. Bob knows it too. There's a laminated poster on the door of the bathroom. He showed it to me, my first day. He said he was CPR certified.

"Bob!"

He nods, lowering his face to Big Nick's. Then he pops up again. "I can't . . . I'm just . . . I can't . . . I can't breathe . . . I—"

He's babbling, and I can feel the panic rising in my chest, but I keep my voice calm as I kneel down on the floor. "Bob, listen to me. You have to. You have to do it."

He turns to me, looking stricken.

"You have to do it," I repeat. "Think about it. This is a life. This . . . is someone's life. You have to do it."

Bob nods. He lowers his face again, and this time he does it. He breathes.

I watch Big Nick's chest rise, and my head feels fuzzy, like I might pass out. "You're doing great," I tell Bob. My voice sounds far away and high-pitched. "I'm going to call

911 now," I say, reaching into my pocket for my cell. "OK? You keep going. You're doing great."

"Clear a path," a gruff voice says.

I look up and there are two gloved hands, reaching out to rip open Big Nick's shirt. A third hand, pressing fingers to his neck. "Sixtysomething male . . . cardiac arrest . . ."

A gurney is rolling through the door.

I stumble to my feet, my legs tingling and heavy as lead pipes, so relieved I could cry.

Bob wouldn't get into the ambulance. He started to; after the paramedics wheeled Big Nick up the ramp, Bob took about five steps forward, then turned right around and walked down.

"I can't," he mumbled to me. "I'm sorry. . . . Hospitals . . . they just . . . I'm sorry. . . . I can't."

"It's OK," I told him. "I'll go."

Now, strapped into the shiny black ambulance seat, I am trying to be helpful, telling the paramedics everything I know. One of them, the woman, has a form. *Name. Address. Next of kin.* Her hair is dishwater blonde and lank-looking, but her eyes are kind. She's patient while I dig through my backpack for the real-estate listing Liv printed out—the one with the Tuccis' house on it.

"Your friend's a diabetic," the woman says. "Did you know that?"

I shake my head.

He was wearing a medic alert bracelet on his wrist; that's how they knew. That's why he was acting so strangely, she explains. He was having a hypoglycemic attack. That's why there's a needle in his arm right now, pumping in insulin.

I nod, a little too vigorously, hurting my neck. *How did I not notice the medic alert bracelet? If I had, I might have been able to—*

"He's lucky you were there," the woman says, as the ambulance flies over a bump. "Otherwise he'd be in a coma."

Lucky. Uh-huh. I am still nodding. *Coma.*

She reaches out to pat my knee. "You did good, honey. You did real good."

"Mom?" I'm calling from the ER lobby. From the pay phone, collect, because cell phones aren't allowed here.

"Josie?"

"Mom?" My voice sounds high and thin. "Mom, I'm in the hospital—"

"The *hospital*? What? Are you—"

"I'm fine," I tell her. "It's not me, it's . . . it's Mr. Tucci. . . . He passed out in Fiorello's. He came in, looking all sweaty and weird, and all of a sudden he just . . ." I pause, swallowing hard. I yank on the silver phone cord, wrapping it around my arm like a bracelet.

"Oh, honey."

"Mom?" I don't even think, I just say it. "Will you come?"

"We'll get in the car right now. It'll be a while—a few hours, at least."

"That's OK. . . . Mom?"

"Yes."

"Thank you."

I put the phone back in its cradle. Letting go, I see that my hand is trembling, just slightly, like I've aged eighty years in five minutes.

I am eating my third HoHo from the vending machine in the lobby when Paul Tucci's mother bursts through the door. I recognize her right away: silver bob, crisp white shirt, khakis. You can tell she was in a big rush to get here, though; she's wearing bedroom slippers. There's mud caked along the bottoms. Everywhere she steps, she leaves a footprint.

I get to observe Mrs. Tucci for a whole twenty minutes while she talks to the nurses. She's asking a lot of questions. I can't hear the words, but I can see her mouth move. She has thin lips, two straight lines, with creases all around.

At one point, the shorter nurse, Patty—I met her when I came in—nods in my direction, and Mrs. Tucci looks over. I squint, pretending to read the clock above her head.

But that doesn't stop her.

She's walking over, leaving one muddy footprint after another in her wake. Now she's standing in front of me, clutching her tan leather purse in both hands. "You saved my husband's life."

My mouth feels sticky suddenly, each tooth encased in HoHo sludge. She doesn't recognize me, from Shop-Co or from anywhere. That much is clear.

"You saved my husband's life," she repeats.

I shake my head.

"You did. They told me."

"It wasn't me," I say. "It was Bob. Bob Schottenstein, from Fiorello's Café. He did the rescue breathing. I just . . . you know . . . called 911. And then the paramedics really—"

She bends down to hug me, her purse thumping against my back. "Thank you." She smells like Lysol. "Thank you. . . . Thank you." She holds on tight for a minute, then stands up straight again, dabbing her eyes with the back of one knuckle.

"You're welcome," I say.

"Christina Tucci," she blurts, shooting out a hand. Long, tapered fingers, no polish.

I nod. My throat is dry. "Josie. Josie Gardner."

It's Liv I'm talking to when the Tucci brothers arrive, all three of them, bursting through the ER doors together, speed walking en masse to the nurses station. "We're looking for Nico Tucci," one of them says.

And another one says, "He's our father."

"Oh my God." I almost drop the phone. "Oh my God. . . . Oh my *God*. OhmyGodohmyGodohmyGod."

"What?" Liv says. "Josie, *what*?"

I turn my back to the nurses station, whisper, "I think my father's here."

Silence.

"Liv?"

"Are you serious?"

"Would I joke about this?"

Another pause. A bigger one. Then, "Holy *shite*, Josie, are you sure?"

"Well, yeah. There are three of them, and they said Big Nick was their dad, so one of them has to be . . ."

"Your dad."

"*Paul*. One of them has to be—"

"Wait," Liv says, cutting me off. "How?"

"What?"

"How could they get there so fast?"

"I don't know."

"I mean, assuming they came from North Carolina, even if they *flew* it would take, like, at least—"

"Who *knows*?" I say. "Who *cares*? The point is, they're here. I'm telling you—"

"That's it, I'm coming to the hospital. Wait right there. Don't *leave*, even if Kate gets there. *Especially* if Kate gets there. Holy shite, Jose. HOLY FRIGGIN' SHITE!"

"I know!"

"I'm coming right now," she says. "As soon as I hang up."

"Well, hang up then."

"OK, I am! Chill!"

Chill? How can I *chill?* How can I do *anything?* I flop back into a chair again, staring at the nurses station. The Tucci brothers are gone. Nurse Patty must have taken them to Big Nick's room to join their mother.

I close my eyes, take a deep breath, let it out again. "Oh my God," I whisper.

It hits me that this is the Before. This moment, right here. Everything that comes next will be the After.

Fourteen

I am in the waiting room, waiting. There are two other people in here: a skinny blonde in Spandex and an iron-on cat sweatshirt, and a sketchy-looking guy with long, greasy hair. I can feel him staring at me, but I am avoiding eye contact.

My mom texted me to say that she and Jonathan are still two hours away; there's a pileup on I-95. Liv will be here any second. That is, unless she's picking out the perfect emergency-room outfit, in which case it's anyone's guess.

I'm not remotely hungry, but here I am in front of the vending machine again, considering the Cheez Doodles. No cheese in there, really. *Cheez*. Which can't be good for anyone.

I walk to the corner of the room, perch myself on the

edge of a hard green chair, one eye locked on the door to the hallway. *Stay where you are, Tuccis*, I think. *Just stay exactly where you are and don't move.* Down the hall, I know, in some antiseptic room, the five of them are gathered.

Josie, is what I told her. *Josie Gardner.*

Is Mrs. Tucci saying my name out loud? Are lightbulbs going on over anyone's head? *Gardner. . . . Gardner. . . . Hey, Paul, remember that girl you dated back in high school? Whatshername? . . .*

No. They are too focused on Big Nick right now. On how he's doing. Big Nick in a hospital bed, hooked up to needles and tubes. There's no reason for them to be thinking about me at all. I could be anyone. Just another teenage girl in a ponytail, perched on a hard green chair, waiting.

I hear footsteps in the hallway, voices.

I stand. I can't help it. I pop straight out of my seat like a jack-in-the-box. Is it them? Paul Tucci and his brothers?

I yank my hair loose from its elastic, pinch my cheeks to make them pink. Cat Sweatshirt and Greaseball are both staring at me, but I don't care. I am picturing the yearbook photo I've seen a thousand times: Paul Tucci at seventeen. His baseball hat, his Tom Cruise nose, his white lopsided grin. If Paul's mom told him about the girl who called 911, he could be coming to meet me. I have to be prepared. I have to be ready to—

"Josie?"

It's Liv, rounding the corner. Liv, in a JUST ADD WATER T-shirt, holding out her arms. "Oh my God, Josie."

Glad though I am to see her, I am also weirdly disappointed.

"Thanks for coming," I mumble into her shoulder. Liv's hug is as familiar to me as the scruffy patchwork quilt on my bed—the one I've slept with since I was three.

"Of course I came! How could I not?" We walk over to the window, scoot two chairs together. "Well?" she says, leaning in close.

"Well what?"

"*Where is he?*" She is whispering, but loudly, like she's onstage.

Cat Sweatshirt stares at us, popping her gum.

"Shhh," I say. "I don't know. I think in Big Nick's room, with everyone else."

"Well, what does he look like? Is he cute?"

I tell her I don't know; I didn't get a good look. Anyway, there were three of them and they were all wearing hats. I couldn't tell which was which.

"What kind of hats?" Liv says.

"Who cares?"

"I do. A hat can say a lot about a person. Like if he's wearing one of those puffy John Deere tractor caps he could be some right-wing nutjob, but if it's just, like, a plain black stocking cap—"

"Liv, I didn't notice. OK? I was a little preoccupied with, you know, the whole *my-dad-showing-up-out-of-nowhere* thing."

She smiles. "You realize you just called him your dad."

"So what! I'm nervous! This whole thing is, like . . . insanity!"

She nods. "I know." She reaches into her back pocket for something. "I brought Altoids."

"I hate those things. They always sound like a good idea. *Curiously Strong Peppermints*. But then you eat one and it burns the taste buds right off your tongue."

"Just take it. It'll distract you."

I stare at the little white pellet in my hand. "Liv?"

"Yeah."

"Paul Tucci is in this building right now. My *father* is in this building right now."

"I know."

"What do I say? I mean, if I see him again."

"You say what you say, Josie."

"Right."

You say what you say. Of course. This is the perfect advice. So organic, so natural. You *say* what you *say.* . . . Right.

While I am pondering this, Liv brings me hot cocoa from the nurses station. It tastes horrible, like chalk and battery acid, warmed to a nauseating fifty-five degrees.

I thank her.

She shrugs. "What can I say? It's a Livaccino."

For the next hour and a half, every hair on my body is standing at alert. My ears perk every time someone walks down the hall. Whenever we hear a male voice, Liv sprints to the doorway, peeks out. Then she slinks back in. "Just a doctor," she tells me. Or, "Just some dude with a mop." Then, the fifth time: "Holy shite."

There is no question in my mind who is coming.

I want to see him, but I don't.

I'm scared, but I'm not.

Liv sprints to the coffee table, grabs two magazines, tosses one to me.

As the Tuccis walk in, we both pretend we are reading.

"Josie?" Mrs. Tucci says. "These are my sons."

I make myself look up, make my mouth crack open. "Hey."

Fifteen

THERE'S NO WAY to tell this story and do it justice. No possible way. But that is what I'm trying to do right now—tell Riggs everything that happened today. Piece it all together for him. Over the phone. At 1:17 a.m.

It's a terrible hour to call someone, I know. I could have waited to see him at school. I could have e-mailed. But I didn't think about that when I was lying in bed, reaching for my phone in the dark. I didn't think at all; I just dialed. Anyway, even though he was asleep when he answered, he sounded glad I called. "Josie," he says, so sweetly. "Jo-sie. Jo-sie."

"Matt."

"Josie." His voice is thick with sleep. "How *are* you?"

"Good. And . . . well, crazy. It was a crazy day."

"Tell me."

"I don't know where to start."

"The beginning?"

"Yeah. OK."

"Or wherever. Start wherever."

"It's . . . OK, here are the CliffsNotes: I wake up, go to work, watch my grandfather go into cardiac arrest, call 911. Then, when we get to the ER, I meet my grandmother for the first time, even though she doesn't know she's my grandmother yet. *Then*, my *father*, who I've never even *seen* except in my mom's high-school yearbook, shows up with his two brothers. They were all at their ski condo in Waterville Valley, see, when they got the call. That's how they got here so—"

"Josie."

"What?"

"Is this fiction or nonfiction?"

I laugh, a tiny croak. All I've told Riggs up until this point are the barest essentials about the Tuccis. I think how ludicrous everything must sound right now, how ludicrous it *is*.

"Josie?"

"Would you believe me if I told you I'm not exaggerating, not even for effect?"

He breathes out. "Whoa."

"Right," I say. "*Whoa* is right."

I close my eyes, lie back on the pillow, and cup the phone to my ear like it's my lifeline—like the hot-water bottles my mom used to give me when I had an ear infection. I start again from the beginning: quietly, calmly, without leaving anything out.

"Oh my God, Matt. You should have seen my mom's face when she walked into the waiting room and they were all sitting there. Can you imagine, just *running into him* like that? And then, it's not only him, it's his whole family? And everyone's looking from me to my mom to Paul to Jonathan. And *Paul's* face? It went, like, completely white. I don't know which of them looked worse. I honestly thought he was going to keel over. And then he's like, 'Katie?' and she's like, 'Hello, Paul.' You could have heard a pin drop in there, I swear to God."

I take a breath, pulling the phone away from my ear, replaying the scene in my head. I picture the stunned look on my mother's face—the moment our eyes met, and the way she opened her mouth, then closed it, then opened it again. I remember thinking, *This is it.* I could feel Liv's hand, warm and strong against mine, as we waited for my mom to say something else.

But nothing came.

Instead, it was Paul who spoke. "Katie . . ." he said. "Is this . . . ?" He was gesturing to me. "Am I . . . ?"

And my mom choked out one word: *Yes.*

"Josie is your daughter!" Liv practically sang out the news, like she was announcing the big winner on *Miss America.*

For a second, the waiting room was dead silent again, except for Mrs. Tucci's sharp intake of breath. Then one of the Tucci brothers, Peter, mumbled, "Jesus Christ." And the other brother, Patrick, said, "Well, it's about time."

Patrick Tucci was slapping Paul Tucci on the back, grinning. He was not following the I-am-completely-shocked protocol. Which could only mean one thing: he already knew. Which was news to *me*.

"Daughter?" Mrs. Tucci spoke slowly, enunciating both syllables. "What do you mean *daughter*?"

And there, right in the middle of the ER waiting room, Paul Tucci said it: "Mom, this is my daughter, Josie." And then, just in case there was any confusion, he cleared it up in the next breath. "Mine and Kate's."

My daughter. Mine and Kate's. . . .

"Matt?" I say now. "Are you still awake?"

"Yeah."

"God, Matt, what do you think was going through his head?"

"Paul's?"

"Yeah. Meeting me—the kid who helped his dad, right? Then, like an hour later, my mom shows up. The girl he used to love. The girl he knocked up, you know? And suddenly, the kid who helped his dad isn't just the kid who helped his dad, it's his daughter. . . . I mean, what could he have been *thinking*, in that moment? What was going through his *head*?"

"I don't know," Riggs says.

"Well, yeah," I say. "How could you?"

"Want to know what's going through *my* head?"

"What?"

"You."

I smile in the dark. "That's sweet."

"*You're* sweet." He lowers his voice. "What are you wearing right now?"

"What?"

"Nightgown or PJs? . . . Something lacy?" He's using his sexy voice—his hook-up voice. Suddenly, all the sweetness has been sucked right out of this conversation.

"Who cares what I'm wearing?"

"I do," he says. "I want to be able to picture you when you're talking."

"I'm trying to tell you something important."

"And I'm trying to tell *you* something important," he says, soft and teasing. "I can't stop thinking about the other night. You, next to me . . ."

"Matt."

"Your skin is amazing . . . so warm . . . I just want to—"

"Matt, God! Is that all you can think about?"

It's clear to me now. Everything I've been saying for the past half hour—about my day, about my dad—has gone in one ear and out the other. Suddenly, I'm too mad to talk anymore.

"Look," I say. "I have to go." I hang up without saying good-bye, without having to hear another word.

I'm so mad, I'm hot all over. It takes me forever to fall asleep.

When I wake up, I remember everything that happened yesterday—Paul Tucci, Matt, all of it—and a tidal wave of feeling crashes over me: disbelief, mixed with nausea.

I find myself standing outside my mother's door, knocking.

"Come in," she says.

So I do.

I expect to find her in a lump under the covers, because it's so early. But she's not. She's sitting up in bed, her bangs in a clip, holding the Paul Tucci yearbook in her lap.

"How did you sleep?" she asks.

I shrug. "Not great."

"That makes two of us," she says, casually sliding the yearbook off her lap, onto the side of the bed farthest from me.

I raise my eyebrows, smirk.

"What?" my mom says.

"You don't have to pretend you weren't looking at his picture."

She waves a hand through the air, like it's no big deal. It's no big deal that the love of her life—the guy who dumped us for another girl—just showed up out of nowhere after sixteen years, finally admitting he's my father.

"Didn't you want to just slap him in the face, right there in front of everyone?"

My mom shakes her head slowly.

"Why *not*?"

"Because . . ." She hesitates. "That's not how I feel."

"Well, how *do* you feel?"

It's the first time I've gotten to ask this question. I wasn't about to open my mouth yesterday, in front of Jonathan, who *of course* was glued to my mother's hip the entire time at the hospital, and who *of course* was waiting in the parking lot when my mom and I came out of the hospital, and who *of course* stayed at our house until God knows what hour last night, until I finally heard the front door slam and his Subaru peel out of the driveway.

Now I am waiting for my mother to tell me how she feels. About Paul Tucci announcing I was his daughter. About seeing him again.

"Honestly?" she says. "My head is pounding. . . . I need coffee."

I give her my blankest stare. Here I am, asking the question to end all questions, wanting to hear the answer to end all answers, and this is what I get. *My head is pounding. I need coffee.*

"*I* know!" my mother says, leaping onto the floor, like lightning just struck the bed. "Let's go out for breakfast!"

"Out for breakfast," I repeat.

"In fact . . ." She grabs the pair of jeans that's been lying in a clump on the rug. "Let's take the whole day off! . . . We haven't had a mother-daughter day in a while. . . . You don't have a game today, do you? Or a test? . . . I'll call in sick to work. . . ."

"Are you OK?" I ask, looking for signs of mental collapse. She's standing in front of the mirror, yanking a brush through her hair. . . . Now she's rifling through her dresser . . . smoothing on a layer of lipstick (she *never* wears lipstick) . . . mascara (ditto).

Finally, she whips around, smiling. "I'll even let you drive!"

OK, it's official. My mother is completely off her nut. Since I got my permit, she has taken me driving exactly five times, and each of those five times she has suffered a small heart attack. Which is why she has left my driving instruction exclusively up to Pops and Dodd, who are so busy teaching Liv, they don't have time for me.

"Seriously?" I say. "I can drive?"

"Sure!" My mom is still smiling. There's lipstick on her tooth, a crazy hot-pink smear.

We've had our Egg McMuffins, and we're back in the car. I know I should be practicing three-point turns and hill starts, but right now I'm just cruising along the back roads between Elmherst and North Haven. My mom is in the passenger seat with coffee in hand. Also, with foot on the invisible brake in front of her, which she presses every thirty seconds.

"Maybe you should downshift, J-Bear?" she says, glancing sideways at me.

I shake my head. "I'm going forty-five. I need to be in fourth."

"Uh-huh." She nods, takes a sip of coffee. "OK. . . . You're doing great."

"I know," I say.

I feel a rush of adrenaline. Riding in a car is so different when you're behind the wheel. *Freeing.* The last place I want to be right now is school, stuck behind a desk, conjugating French verbs. I'm also glad not to have to deal with the Riggs situation. What is he thinking right now, I wonder. Does he feel bad about last night? A small, mean part of me hopes that he is suffering—wants him to be waiting at my locker between every class period today, panicked over my absence, worried that he's about to be dumped. I'm not *planning* on dumping him. But I don't mind letting him sweat a little. . . .

"Josie!" My mother lets out a shriek, as I swerve to avoid a crossing squirrel.

"Relax," I say, downshifting to third.

"I'm *trying.*"

We're both trying. All morning, we have been. Since leaving the house, neither of us has acknowledged what happened yesterday, but you can feel it all around us. A big gray cloud of Tucci is gathering in the air above our heads, growing bigger by the second, filling up the car. We can pretend that the tension is about my driving, but it's not.

"Josie!" My mother slams on her invisi-brake. "Shift!"

"I *am!*" Does she think I can't anticipate a simple stop sign? *Sheesh.* . . . I downshift to second, then first. I flip on my blinker and turn—quite smoothly, I might add—onto Campbell Road.

I glance over at my mom, cocking an eyebrow at her. *See? I rock.* But she isn't looking at me; she's looking at the rearview mirror, frowning. "Crap."

"What," I say. But she doesn't have to answer because I can see for myself—the swirling strobe of blue light behind us.

Before I can ask what I did wrong, my mother orders me to pull over. Like I'm a moron. Like I've never seen a police car before.

"I *know,*" I say, disguising my panic with annoyance.

It is exactly how you would imagine it: Cop, stepping out of his cruiser, one shiny black boot at a time. Swaggering over, slowly, belly first, to intimidate you; hoisting up his gun belt with one hand and lowering his Ray-Bans with the other. Glaring into your open window with thick jet-black eyebrows. "You do realize that was a stop sign back there."

I clear my throat. "Yes, sir."

"You do realize you rolled through it."

Um . . . no.

Big, heavy sigh. "License and registration."

Nodding, I reach into the back pocket of my jeans for my learner's permit, which thank God I remembered to bring, then awkwardly across to the glove box, to dig out the registration card. I wouldn't have to do this if my mother would help. But no. She is slouched down in her seat, gazing out the opposite window, refusing to even look at me.

Thanks for the support, Kate.

"Here you go," I say, handing over the paperwork, polite as can be.

Officer Eyebrows grunts, looks down at my permit. Then he looks up again. "You need to be accompanied by a licensed driver age twenty-one or over."

I hesitate, then say, "I am. That's my mom."

He pokes his bristly, flattopped head through the window. "Ma'am?" Then, because my mother doesn't respond, he says it again, louder. "*Ma'am?* I need to see your driver's license."

Somehow my mother manages to duck between her legs and come up with her license but keep her head down, like she's suddenly morphed into one of those double-jointed circus performers.

"*Mom,*" I say. "*God.*"

I hand over her license, while she remains in pretzel position. Like a complete freak.

"Katharine Gardner?" Officer Eyebrows says.

"Yes?" The word floats up, but the head stays down.

"Uh, ma'am? . . . I need to see your face. . . ."

My own face burns. What the *hell* is she doing? As if getting pulled over isn't humiliating enough, my mother has to go all—

"Ma'am?"

"Mom." I poke her spine with my finger. Once . . . twice. . . . I'm about to do it a third time, when she finally decides to pop up. By the look of her face, you'd think she's just finished running a marathon. Her cheeks are bright red and her forehead is shiny with sweat.

Officer Eyebrows glowers at her. Then, suddenly, those two furry black caterpillars shoot straight to the top of his forehead. His mouth forms an "O" of surprise. *"Katie?* Katie *Gardner?"*

"Uh-huh," my mom says weakly.

"Katie Gardner, holy shit! . . . I never knew you were a Katharine. . . ." He's grinning now, whipping off the Ray-Bans. "It's me, Sully! . . . From high school!"

For a second my mom pretends to be confused, unable to place him, which is downright hilarious because even I know who he is.

Sully.

Aka Tom Sullivan.

Aka Paul Tucci's BFF, the one person decent enough to break the news to my mother about the infamous Arizona girlfriend, because Paul Tucci, aka Spineless Wanker, didn't have the guts.

"Sully," he repeats. "*You* know . . ."

Now my mom is nodding, trying to smile but not quite pulling it off. "Sully! Of course! . . . How *are* you?"

He gives his spiel. He's still living in North Haven. Blah, blah, blah. He's a cop. Blah, blah, blah. He married Anna-beth Reese, from high school. They have two boys. Blah, blah, blah. . . .

"Katie Gardner," he says now, shaking his head. "*Damn*. . . . How long has it been? Fifteen years? I don't think I've seen you since . . ." He pauses for a minute. "Since you were . . . well . . ."

"With child?" I blurt, surprising myself.

The eyebrows shift to me.

I shrug. "I'm . . . *you* know . . ."

My mom makes a strangled noise in the back of her throat, but it's not her reaction I'm trying to gauge. It's Sully's.

"No kidding." He is looking at me, squinting. "Uh-huh. You look just like your dad." To my mom, he says, "She looks just like Tooch."

My mother lets out a squeak, like a mouse.

"You think?" I say.

Sully nods. "Spitting image."

For a moment, in my semi-emboldened state, I forget

that I'm talking to the cop who pulled me over. All I want is information. And I don't care if my mom is wigging out beside me either. I need to know.

"So," I say, "do you see him much?"

"Tooch?... Shit, I haven't seen Tooch since high school.... After he moved, he just ... I don't know ... dropped off the face of the earth. . . ." Sully hesitates, glances at my mom. "You heard from him?" His expression is sincere, not mocking. He really wants to know.

My mom shrugs, licks her lips. "Actually, he's in town. I ... saw him yesterday. . . ." She looks like she's debating saying more, but doesn't.

Sully's mouth is hanging slightly open. "Are you guys . . . ?"

My mom laugh-snorts. "No."

"Right." He laughs too, like he sees her point. The prospect of a Tooch-Katie rekindling is simply too crazy to contemplate. "So . . . what? You're not still single, are you? . . . I mean, no *way* are you still single. . . ."

My cheeks burn, hearing this. They burn for my mom, at what Sully is implying. As if she would waste sixteen years of her life pining over her asshole high-school boyfriend.

"*Actually,*" I say loudly, "she's in a very serious relationship. His name is Jonathan, and he's a *very* talented musician."

I don't look at my mom. I keep my eyes directly on Sully, whose "Oh, yeah?" sounds seriously lame.

"*Very* talented," I repeat.

I am lying, but who knows, Jonathan may actually *be* a very talented musician. I've never bothered asking him to show me his instrument collection, let alone to play me anything. . . .

Anyway, the point is, nobody calls my mom pathetic. Nobody. I don't care who you are. Or how shiny your badge is.

Sixteen

MEETING OFFICER SULLY is just what I needed to get my courage up. This is what I realize, as soon as I drive off—not with a ticket, but with a stern warning not to roll through any more stop signs. The logic is twisted, but somehow, facing Sully has given me the guts to face my father. I mean *really* face him—not like yesterday, when I barely said two words in his presence.

I need to do it now. Before I lose my nerve.

"*What?*" my mom says when I tell her. I don't mention Paul's name. She is still in recovery mode after seeing Sully, and I don't want to send her over the edge. All I say is we're driving to the hospital.

"*Why?*"

"I want to stop by the gift shop to pick up some flowers.

For Big Nick. . . . And, you know . . . see how he's feeling."

Silence from the passenger's seat.

"Come on," I say. "It's what you *do*. When someone's in the hospital, you bring flowers. It's not a big deal."

"Uh-huh," she says.

"I'm not saying you have to come with me. You can wait in the car if you want."

"OK."

"OK you'll come, or OK you'll wait in the car?"

"I'll wait in the car," she says. Then, quietly, "I just can't deal with seeing Paul's mother again."

"His *mother*? Why?"

I can understand her not wanting to deal with Paul, but Mrs. Tucci? I actually thought she handled herself pretty well yesterday, all things considered. Sure, she was shocked to find out Paul had a kid, but come on, who wouldn't be?

"Please." My mom snorts. "Did you not see the way she was looking at me the whole time? . . . She hates me, Josie. She always has."

"I'm sure she doesn't *hate* you."

"Yes, she does. She *never* thought I was good enough for Paul. And now . . . the golden boy and the high-school tramp have a baby? . . . It's like her worst nightmare—"

"She *hugged* me," I say defensively.

"Well, of course she hugged you. You saved her husband's life."

"That was the *first* hug, before she found out. She hugged me *again*, after. And the only reason she didn't stick around to talk was that nurse came and got her. . . ."

"Whatever."

"Don't you think you're being a bit harsh? Her husband almost *died*. And then, she finds out her son has been keeping this gigantic secret for, like, years. . . ."

"Why are you defending her?"

"I'm not *defending* her. I'm just saying—"

"Josie!" She grabs the dashboard. "Jesus!" Another squirrel has just crossed our path, interrupting our moment. Which I don't mind in the least. Because my mother is really starting to get on my nerves.

"Excuse me," I say to the curly-haired nurse who is sitting at the nurses station, reading *Us* magazine.

I'm glad I decided on sunflowers instead of tulips; sunflowers are stronger. Manlier. . . .

"Excuse me?" I say again.

Big Nick isn't critical anymore; he's stable, which is why I'm in a different wing from yesterday. The recovery wing. Not, apparently, a wing that prides itself on customer service. . . .

"*Excuse me*," I say, for yet a third time.

"*What*," the nurse says, not looking up from her magazine.

"I'm looking for Nico Tucci's room."

"*Who?*"

"Nico Tucci?"

Now she looks up, not so much at me, but at the clock over my head. "Only ten minutes left in visiting hour."

"That's OK. I just wanted to drop off—"

"Relation?"

"Excuse me?"

"*Re-la-tion,*" she says, like I'm the village idiot. "How are you *re-la-ted* to the patient? It's relatives only."

"Oh. . . . I didn't know. I—"

"Granddaughter," comes a deep voice behind me.

I whip around and there is Patrick, the pilot brother, holding a tray of coffees in one hand and a paper bag in the other.

"He's her grandfather, Gwen," he says, leaning in and winking at the nurse. "Stop being such a bitch. Here"—he plops the bag on the desk in front of her—"I brought you a cruller."

She smiles at him. Incredibly. "Are you trying to make me fat?"

He laughs. "Couldn't do that if I tried, sweetheart."

I feel a hand grab my elbow and now here we are, me and Uncle Pat, gliding down the hall together toward a bank of elevators.

"Don't mind Gwen," he says low. "Her bark is worse

than her bite. Anyway, she's just jealous because you're pret-
tier than she is. You got your old man's looks." He winks at
me, presses the Up arrow. "Pete's the brain. I'm the jock. But
Paulie? Paulie hit the jackpot. . . ."

My eyelid is twitching. I can't think of a thing to say.
Not a single word.

"Hey," Patrick says gently, as we step onto the elevator.
"You OK?"

I nod.

He looks at me, and the words pour out of his mouth.
"I feel responsible, in a way. . . . Pete and I both do. . . .
When Paul first told us Katie was pregnant, we were away at
college . . . living it up, you know, not exactly at the height
of maturity. . . . Paulie was really torn up about it, though.
He wanted to do the right thing. Tell the parents, propose,
whatever it took. When Katie decided not to keep the baby
and they had that huge fight and broke up, right before our
folks moved to Arizona, Pete and I told him, *Listen, man,
maybe this is for the best. You've got college to think about . . .
your whole future ahead of you . . .*"

He keeps talking, but all I can hear are those same six
words, over and over again. *Decided not to keep the baby. Decided not to keep the baby.*

My mind is spinning. As the elevator dings and the doors
open, Patrick turns to me and I don't even wait to hear what
he's going to say next. I just shove the flowers into his chest.
"I have to go."

"But—"

I stumble blindly out of the elevator and down the hall, walking as fast as I can, to the nearest exit sign.

"Josie! Wait!"

But I don't wait. I walk faster and faster, until I'm running. Through the hall, down the stairs, out the door, across the parking lot to the car where my mother is waiting.

"That was fast," she says, when I open the door.

I stare at her. I stare and I stare.

"Why did you break up?"

She frowns for a moment, then says, "What?"

"You and Paul Tucci. Before he moved away. You had a fight and you broke up. Why?"

"Oh, Josie. That was a long time ago—"

"I know exactly how long ago it was. You were pregnant with me. Why did you break up?"

"Josie, I don't know what you're—"

"Patrick told me," I cut her off. "So don't even think about lying. *Why did you break up?* I want to hear you say it."

"I don't know." She's looking down at her lap now, shaking her head. "We had a fight. I don't—"

"Yes, you do," I snap. "Tell me."

"Josie, how I felt then has nothing to do with how I—"

"You're stalling. Tell me. Tell me why you broke up. Tell me."

"I'm trying to!"

"No, you're not!"

"*I wanted to have an abortion! OK? Is that what you wanted to hear? I was sixteen years old and I didn't want to be pregnant! Paul wanted to keep the baby and I didn't and that's why we broke up!*"

Her yelling makes me jump, but I don't back down.

"He thought you were getting an abortion. He *moved*, thinking you were getting an abortion. . . . And then—what—you just *changed your mind*? You changed your mind and you didn't think he deserved to *know*? That's why I never heard from him, isn't it? Because you never told him. You never even told him he had a kid, and he was the one who wanted to keep it. He wanted the baby and you didn't. *He* wanted me."

The expression on her face is horrifying, but I don't care.

"No," she is saying, shaking her head. "No. . . . Josie, listen to me. You are my *life*."

But I am not listening. I am opening the car door, and I am slamming it in her face. I am sprinting across the parking lot, sprinting as fast as I can because I need to get away from her.

I need to get to school.

I need Liv.

It's twelve thirty—the middle of fifth period—by the time the PVTA bus drops me off. Now I am standing outside AP

English, trying to flag down Liv without Mrs. Montrose no-
ticing.

Finally I do, and Liv gets a bathroom pass.

In the hall, I don't have to say a word. She takes one look
at my face and she knows. "Something happened."

I nod.

"Tucci-related?"

I nod again.

"Tell me."

I can feel my eyes filling with tears and my chin quiver-
ing slightly. I know that if I open my mouth I'll start bawling
hysterically in the middle of the junior corridor, which is the
last thing I want to do.

"OK," Liv says gently, getting it. "OK." She tells me that
the bell is about to ring for lunch. She tells me it's burgers
and tater tots and if we're first in line, Lynette the lunch lady
will give us extra. "Grease," Liv says, "is good for the soul."

I nod, making a little whimpering sound.

She slings an arm around my shoulders as we walk down
the hall. "Whenever you're ready," she says, "just tell me who
needs a slap upside the head, and I will do the honors."

Somehow I make it through the rest of the day. I didn't think
I'd be able to focus on school, but it is actually a good distrac-
tion. Equations, not abortions. *Mansfield Park*, not mothers
who wish you were never born. Then, as I am walking to the

girls' locker room to get dressed for practice, I spot Riggs entering the guys' locker room, and I get mad all over again.

Liv is at her locker, pulling socks over her shin guards.

"I'm not going to practice," I say low, even though it's so loud in here right now, no one would hear us anyway. Music is blasting and Jamie and Schuyler are showing off the stripper moves they learned at some pole-dancing class at their gym.

Liv looks at me, eyebrows raised.

"I just can't deal right now," I mumble. "Tell Coach I'm sick or something. I need to get out of here."

"So," she says out of the side of her mouth, "let's get out of here."

"We?"

"I'll take you anywhere you want to go."

"What do you mean you'll *take* me—"

"I had my driver's test this morning, so . . ."

"*What?* You never told me you were—"

"Yes, I did."

"No, you didn't."

"Yes, Josie, I did. You've just been a *lit-tle* self-involved lately. But I forgive you . . . because I passed."

"You did?"

Liv crooks her finger for me to come closer, then reaches into her gym bag, pulls out a key ring, and grins. "You're looking at a licensed driver."

"Oh my God, Liv!"

"I know! I have Dodd's car!"

"He gave you the Beamer?"

"Yeah. Just for the day. . . . Come on."

"But—"

"No *buts*, Josie. We're going."

She yanks my hand and I follow. No one even notices us leave.

Five minutes later, here we are, gunning it out of the parking lot. If you're going to blow off soccer practice, it's a good idea to have Little Miss Honor Society by your side, instead of, say, Chuck Bikofsky, who's been smoking pot since the third grade.

I know Coach will be pissed when we don't show up, but I feel strangely calm about what we're doing. Liv is a good driver. Confident. . . . Then I remember why we're leaving—everything Matt said, and Patrick said, and my mother said—and I feel sick. The farther we drive, the deeper the pit in my stomach. I have to do something to get rid of this feeling or I'm going to barf.

I tell Liv to pull over.

"Now?"

"Now."

"OK," she says and steers the car up over a curb, onto a patch of grass next to some woods. She cuts the engine and turns to me and I tell her. When I get to the real punch line of the story—the abortion part—something in her face changes and she looks away.

"I mean do you see the freaking *irony* here, Liv? . . . The one person who wanted to keep me doesn't get to, and the one who gets stuck raising me . . . well, she never wanted me in the first place."

"It's not that simple," Liv says to the window.

"You're a mind reader now?" I say.

"No. I just know."

"How?"

"When I thought I was pregnant . . . I *wasn't*, I know, but if I *had been* . . . Josie, there's no question in my mind what I would have done, and I wouldn't have been able to tell my best friend."

"What are you talking about?"

"I would have had to make up some story about miscarrying or falling down the stairs or something. I couldn't have told you the truth."

I stare at her. "Of course you could have told me the truth."

"No, I couldn't. Look how you feel about Kate, almost doing the same thing."

"What? You think I would have judged you because of my *mom*? You think I would have tried to talk you out it?"

She shakes her head. "I don't know."

"I wouldn't have!"

"Josie, what your mom went through . . . the decision she had to make . . . you don't know—you *can't* know unless you've been there."

"I think I know my own mother."

"Listen to me. It's not like that. And it's not about her wanting you or not wanting you. There *was* no you. You were just a clump of cells."

Thanks, Liv.

You would think that this point would be enough, but no; she is just getting warmed up.

"When you can see your whole life stretched out ahead of you and then one morning you wake up and you think you're pregnant and you can't see that life anymore, it's . . . I can't explain the feeling. . . . But Kate had to face that, Josie—*really* face it, not just hypothetically. And she had to face it without a crystal ball telling her what would happen if she made one choice over the other. And maybe the pressure she was getting from Paul didn't help; maybe it made everything worse."

Liv pats my knee. "There," she says. "I've said my piece."

"You have to stop watching Dr. Steve," I tell her.

"Pops finally got TiVo. I can watch every episode now."

"God help us."

"We should blow off practice more often. I think we've made some real progress here."

I snort. Then it hits me. "What do you think Coach is going to do to us?"

Liv shrugs, turning the key in the ignition. "Just a warning. I mean, it's not like we *do* this sort of thing. This was our first offense. . . ." She pulls off the grass and onto the road, formulating her counterargument as she drives—everything she's planning to tell Coach tomorrow, to justify our actions. This is classic Liv. I don't mind listening to her; anything is better than rehashing what happened with my mother and Paul and Matt and everything.

"Great," I mutter ten minutes later as Liv pulls into my driveway.

"What?"

"That," I say, pointing to the car that's parked in my mom's spot. The rusty beige Subaru with the I BRAKE FOR MOZART bumper sticker.

"Sweet ride," Liv says.

I grunt.

There's no mistaking who's on my front porch right now, sitting on the top step. Sandy hair, suede jacket. Funky green sneakers poking out of khaki legs. The only question is, where's his little blonde sidekick?

"Ladies and gentlemen," Liv says, whipping out an imaginary microphone. "The man, the myth, the musical legend . . . *DJ . . . Jazzy . . . Jonathaaaan!*"

"Hilarious," I say.

"Why is he on your porch?"

I shrug.

"Where's Kate?"

"Gee, I don't know . . . an abortion clinic? A *liars' convention*?"

Liv shoots me a look.

"What?"

Jonathan must have spotted me because now he's standing, looking over at the driveway.

"Well," Liv says, glancing at her watch, "I'd love to join your little duet, but . . ."

"Liv. You are *not* leaving me alone with him."

"I have to get the car back. . . ."

"*Liv.*"

"I promised Dodd! It's my first day out, and if I ever want to drive again I have to—"

"Fine," I mutter, reaching for the door handle.

"Call me later," Liv says, leaning over to kiss my shoulder. "I want to hear *everything*."

And then she deserts me.

Crap, I am thinking as I walk across the lawn toward the porch.

Crappity crap.

Big, steaming pile of crap on a stick.

The closer I get to Jonathan, the worse he looks. Slumped shoulders. Bags under the eyes. He's like a puppy that's been kicked, and, truth be told, I feel a twinge of sympathy. If I'd been the one to run into the ex of the person I was dating—

and that ex's entire family—I might look the same way. I might go slamming out of houses and peeling out of driveways in the middle of the night too.

"Hey," I say, as nicely as I can.

"Hey," he says. Then, "I'm looking for your mom."

"She works on Mondays."

He shakes his head. "That's the first place I checked. She called in sick, they said. Early this morning."

"Yeah . . . she's not sick. She . . . we . . . went back to the hospital. You know, to check on Mr. Tucci."

"Oh," Jonathan says. "Uh-huh."

The expression on his face is so miserable I have to ask, "Are you OK?"

"I just . . . need to talk to her."

"Did you try her cell?"

"About a hundred times. She isn't picking up. Do you know where else she could be?"

I shake my head. "I don't. I'm sorry."

Well, this isn't exactly true. I *might* know where she is, if I bothered to check my voice mail. Ever since I booked it out of the parking lot this morning she's been calling and leaving messages. I've just chosen to ignore them.

Jonathan looks at his watch. "I've been waiting here for two hours. . . . I canceled my afternoon lessons. . . . I don't know why. Well, I *do* know why. I . . . I'm crazy about your mom, Josie, and . . . I don't want to lose her."

"Oh," I say. "Uh-huh."

I am cringing so hard right now.

"This happened to me once already, in college. . . ." Jonathan shifts his eyes to the yard, staring out at nothing. "Amy Hahn. We went out for two years and then, out of nowhere, her ex-boyfriend shows up for homecoming and . . . never mind." He laughs, a short bark. "I can't believe I'm telling you this. . . ."

I can't believe it either. I would like nothing more than to jackhammer a hole in the porch and dive through it.

I have no idea where my mother is right now, but I'll tell you one thing: I cannot stay here, having this torturous conversation—

"Will you come with me? To look for her?"

"No," I say. The last person I want to see right now is my mother.

Jonathan looks like I just punched him in the stomach.

"But I *will* take you to do something else. . . . If you let me drive."

"What?"

I shrug. "It's a fair trade. You give me your car keys. I take you somewhere fun, to get your mind off my mom."

I can't believe I'm suggesting this. I must be completely mental. But . . . I feel for the guy. And also, there's no way I'm staying on this porch.

"OK," Jonathan says. Incredibly. He reaches into the pocket of his suede jacket, pulls out his keys, and hands them to me.

*   *   *

Twenty minutes later, we are in the back room of the Pizza Palace, playing video games. In middle school, Liv and I used to come here all the time. Whenever one of us had a crappy day, the other one would say, *You need the Palace.* I reached Level 5 on Super Mario Bros. the day I farted doing a handstand in gym. Liv can attest to this; she still has the chart she made of all our humiliating moments in seventh and eighth grade and which video games we played to make ourselves feel better.

Jonathan is great at video games, as most guys are. He throttles me at Pac-Man and Donkey Kong. So I move us on to Virtual Boogie, because—despite my questionable talent on an actual dance floor—I am a virtual boogie *machine.*

I have already racked up 200,000 boogie points when Jonathan takes over the mat. And he is hilarious. If I were in seventh grade and I were watching him across the arcade, I would think, *What a dork.* In fact, a cluster of girls over by Skee Ball *is* watching; they're wearing their super-low jeans and drinking their supersized sodas and laughing hysterically. Because Jonathan is dorking out, big-time. His feet are moving at warp speed, his arms are flying every which way, and his mouth is forming this crazy "O" shape the whole time.

I don't know why this makes me like him more, but it does. I am thinking, *How many grown men would do this, voluntarily, without alcohol?*

Now Jonathan has hopped off the mat and is shaking his head around like a big, wet dog, sending sweat beads flying everywhere. It's completely disgusting.

"You," I say, "need to hydrate."

After a visit to 7-Eleven, we are back in the car. I let Jonathan drive, so I can focus on the task at hand. "I can't believe you've never had a Slurpee before," I say, sucking hard on my straw so that red slush shoots up into my mouth, exploding against the back of my throat, coating it in ice. *Ahhh.*

"Deprived child," Jonathan says. "My parents were health nuts. No sugar. . . . No artificial colors. . . ."

"You think Blue Woo-Hoo! Vanilla isn't found in nature?" I ask. "Come on. . . ."

He turns to me, smiling a little. His lips are turquoise.

"See?" I say. "Slurpees are good for what ails you."

"Well . . ."

"You're loving it. Admit it."

"OK," he says, sticking the straw back in his mouth. "I admit it. . . . Now I want to introduce *you* to something. . . ."

"What?"

"Not *what*. *Who*." Jonathan reaches out, presses a bunch of buttons on the stereo. Then he pauses, one finger hovering in the air. "Josie?"

"Yeah?"

"Prepare to have your mind blown."

"Oh, God," I say.

"Better than God," he says. "Better than *Slurpees*." He presses Play. "John Coltrane."

When we get back to the house, my mother is still not there. Before Jonathan can lose his John Coltrane high, I reassure him.

"Listen," I say, as we're walking across the lawn toward the porch. "About my mom . . . I don't think you have to worry."

Of course, these words are based on nothing. Because what do I know? I know squat. I am only saying what I would want to hear right now, if I were him.

"Really?" he says. I can see the mixture of hope and doubt in the crinkles of his forehead.

"Really," I say.

Because clearly I don't have eyes in the back of my head. Clearly I can't see my mom's car pulling into the driveway behind Jonathan's Subaru, or the red SUV pulling in behind her. I can't see who's getting out. I can't see the two of them opening their separate doors and closing them. I can't see this: My mother and Paul Tucci, strolling across the lawn toward us. Side by side.

I only turn around when I see the look on Jonathan's face. Like a kid who's just dropped his ice-cream cone.

"Josie," my mom says. Her arms are outstretched. When

she gets to the top step she hugs me: a long-lost-daughter hug.

"What's up?" I am trying to sound cool while the voice inside my head is screaming, WHAT THE %&*#?!

Paul Tucci is on our porch.

Paul Tucci is wearing jeans with a rip in the knee, and hiking boots, and he is on our porch.

Maybe this isn't really happening. Maybe it's a dream—a hallucination brought on by the physical trauma of one hundred squat thrusts. Maybe if I close my eyes and open them, he will disappear. . . .

Close. . . . Open. . . .

Nope.

"Josie," my mother says again. She's stopped hugging me and has pulled away just enough to stare into my eyes. "I'm sorry."

She's sorry.

"For what?" I mumble.

The sky is getting dark, but the porch lights have kicked on, so everyone is illuminated. Paul Tucci has great skin—olive-toned, the kind that tans perfectly in summer. My mom is pale and burns. I am somewhere in the middle.

In my peripheral vision I can see Paul and Jonathan size each other up. This is what guys do. I remember seeing it on the playground in fourth grade. A new kid, Ryan Lounsberry, had come into our class and during recess all the dodgeball boys lined up along the bushes, checking him out. Ryan was short, unlike the coolest boy in our class, Willy Meyer, but there was a beefy cockiness about Ryan, and it took all of five minutes before the two of them were rolling around in the dirt, pummeling the crap out of each other.

Not that this would happen here. Jonathan isn't exactly the boxing type. He's skinny, for one thing. And anyway, all you have to do is look at his car. In addition to braking for Mozart, his message to the world is, NO NUKES! NO WARS!

You could imagine Paul Tucci throwing a punch, though. He's got that square-jaw thing working for him, and muscles you can see through his shirt. It's almost November, but he doesn't bother wearing a coat. His *job* is scaling walls and zip-lining through the North Carolina jungle with juvenile delinquents. He could take Jonathan down in one swing. . . .

But no.

Peaceful and civilized, Paul Tucci is holding out a hand for Jonathan to shake.

Which Jonathan accepts—briefly—before announcing, "I need to talk to Kate." He turns to my mother. "I need to talk to you."

My mom hesitates, and for a second I think she's going to say no. But then she nods. "Let's go inside." She fumbles around in her bag for her keys, then clicks the door open. "We'll be inside," she says to me, like I didn't hear her the first time.

As she and Jonathan enter the house, I notice his hand

fly out to perch in the curve of her back. She's wearing her best jeans, low-riders, that hug her butt just right. Paul Tucci's eyes zoom in, like magnets to metal, and I think, *You're damn right she looks good.* Then, *Stop looking at her, asshole. You have no right to look at her.*

This spark of anger makes my mouth pop open. "Why are you here?"

"It's pretty funny," Paul Tucci says. "Actually. . . . I ran into your mom at the Mobile station. . . . I told her I wanted to talk to you, and she said I could follow her to your house, so . . ."

"Why?"

"I never knew where you lived."

"No, why did you want to talk to me?"

"Oh . . ." He hesitates, clears his throat. He gestures to the pair of wicker chairs beside the porch swing. "OK if we sit?"

I shrug. "Whatever."

Sitting in one chair while Paul Tucci sits in the other, it hits me that this is really happening.

My father is here, on my front porch.

This could be the biggest moment of my life.

And I don't have a clue what to do with it.

I want to ask a million questions, but I don't know where to start. I guess he's feeling the same way, because he keeps clearing his throat, and there's a nervous tic thing happening with his foot.

"How's your dad?" I blurt, filling the silence.

"Good." He nods, relieved. "Much better, thanks. The doctors say he can go home tomorrow, with some new kind of insulin pump. And, you know, swearing on the Holy Bible he'll never eat chocolate again. . . ."

"Right," I say, forcing a chuckle.

More silence.

Then, I have to ask. "So . . . did you tell him?"

Paul clears his throat, nods. "Yeah. . . . Last night, after you and your mom left. . . . You know what he said?" He imitates Big Nick's big booming voice. "'I *knew* there was a reason I liked that Josie girl.'"

"No, he didn't."

"He did. I swear to God."

I snort at the sheer absurdity of what I'm hearing. "Right. He just *rolled with the news* that his son has been *lying his ass off* for sixteen years and now, suddenly, the kid who's been serving him cocoa is his granddaughter! No big deal! . . . Give me a fucking break."

Paul looks startled. Then embarrassed. Good.

"It *is* a big deal," he says quietly. "It's a very big deal. Believe me, I know that, and . . . I should have told my parents sooner."

"*You should have told your parents sooner?*" My voice is hard, furious. "That's all you can say for yourself?"

"No. No, it's not . . ." He's shaking his head. Shake, shake, shake. But no words come out of his mouth.

More throat clearing and foot jiggling.

Both of us stare out at the darkening yard.

Minutes tick by. Or are they hours?

Finally, he speaks. "You have no idea how many times I thought about coming back here."

"Is that right." My tone is cool. Neutral.

"I even bought a plane ticket once. I was in college by then, so you were probably, I don't know . . . a year old?"

I look at him. "What?"

"Well, I was a freshman, it was spring semester . . . you were born in June . . . so you would have been . . . *not quite* one. . . . I bought a plane ticket, to come and see you and your mom, but I never—"

"Wait," I say. My heart has stopped. Literally. It is no longer beating. "You knew about me then?"

He looks at me, surprised.

"You knew my mom didn't go through with the abortion?"

He nods. "Yeah."

"How?" I say. "How did you know?"

He hesitates, frowning slightly. "She sent me a letter. The only letter I ever got."

I don't know what to say. I am speechless. So I say nothing. I let him keep talking.

"Katie's parents, your grandparents, they made it clear to me . . . even when we were dating . . . your grandmother, especially . . . they didn't like me. . . ."

I stare at him. "*So?*"

"*So*, the minute I got Katie's letter telling me she'd decided to keep the baby, I called her house, and your grandmother was the one who answered. 'Katie doesn't want to talk to you, Paul,' she told me. 'She doesn't want to see you. She doesn't want you in this baby's life now, or ever. We don't need your help.' I kept calling, though, even after she said, 'If you continue to call here I will contact the police.' I didn't stop calling, though. Not until the phone was disconnected. And I didn't stop writing, either, until the letters started coming back to me, address unknown."

Letters? What letters?

"I didn't know where they moved," Paul Tucci says. He gestures to the front door. "Here, I guess."

"What letters?" I say out loud.

He looks surprised, but then he shrugs. "Your mom probably threw them out a long time ago. She just didn't tell you."

I sit up straight. "No."

He raises his eyebrows.

"We tell each other everything," I say. "We share *everything*. We don't keep secrets." As I am saying this I am realizing that it's not really true. It is, in fact, a bald-faced lie. My mother *has* been keeping secrets—lots of them. But I keep going. "I know all about your Arizona girlfriend, by the way, so don't even pretend you're the innocent victim here. . . ."

"My what?"

I scoff. "Please. Did you think she wouldn't find out?"

Paul gives me a puzzled look. "Find out *what*?"

"That you ditched her, the minute you moved! The minute you got to Arizona you started dating some other girl! . . .
Your best friend Sully told her everything. At least *he* had the
decency—"

"My best friend Sully."

"Yeah."

"Uh-huh. Did your mom ever tell you what happened
with her and my best friend Sully?"

"No," I say. "What?" My stomach drops the tiniest bit.
"Did they hook up or something?"

"Not exactly. . . . But he tried."

I listen to Paul tell me the story of some high-school
party, a few months before he moved. How he walked into a
room to find Sully putting the moves on my mom. Her pushing him away.

"No *way*," I say. "Did they see you?"

"Sully did," Paul says. "Your mom was . . . well, she'd had
a few drinks. . . . He was definitely taking advantage of the
situation."

"Asshole," I mutter.

Paul gives me a wry smile. "Let's just say that when it
comes to Katie Gardner, Tom Sullivan has never been the
most objective source of information."

Oh my God. *That* explains Officer Eyebrows and his *No-way-are-you-still-single* comment. He wasn't mocking my mom; he was flirting with her.

"He liked her!"

Paul snorts. "He *more* than liked her. He threw his best friend under a bus for her."

I picture a PVTA, a Paul Tucci pancake covered in tire tracks.

"There wasn't an Arizona girlfriend," Paul says. "Just a girl that I was hanging out with. Platonically."

"So Sully lied."

"Sully exaggerated."

"And my mom believed him."

"Apparently."

"Why?"

Paul shakes his head. "I don't know. All I got was the one letter. I never heard from her after that."

"But she loved you!"

"I know," he says. Then, quietly, "I loved her too. I was . . . really happy when I heard she was keeping the baby. I wrote back right away, telling her so. I kept writing too. Even though she never wrote back."

"You're lying," I say, although I'm not sure he is. "There were no letters."

I stand up.

"Josie, wait." He stands too. "I tried. I really did. . . . I called. I wrote. Fifty letters I must have written. But your mom, either she believed Sully, or . . . I don't know . . . All I know is I never heard from her again."

I shake my head. "I don't believe you."

"It's the truth."

I hate when you think your life is one way—when you spend sixteen years accepting certain facts—and it turns out that everything you believed was a myth. I particularly hate when that myth is standing right here next to you on your front porch, telling you something you weren't prepared to hear.

"Why should I believe you?" I say. I'm directing my question to the floor, where the paint is peeling away in gray dandrufflike flakes. Every summer my mom says she's going to scrape it all off and start over, but she never does. "I don't even *know* you."

"I know," Paul says. Then, "Josie."

His hand is on my elbow.

Paul Tucci's hand is on my elbow.

My dad's hand—

"I want you to leave." The words come out strangled, like there's glue in my throat. "Please."

"OK." He drops his hand, nods. "If you change your mind . . . if you want to reach me . . ." I hold my breath as he slides his hand into the back pocket of his jeans and pulls out a business card. "Here," he says.

I take it.

"Anytime, Josie. I mean that. I'll be in town for the next week or so."

I nod, silent. I can't find the words.

He hesitates, then turns and walks down the stairs. Across the grass, onto the driveway, and into the red SUV.

I realize, watching him drive off, that he didn't choose to leave. I'm the one who made him go.

Seventeen

IT TAKES A long time for my mom and Jonathan to finish their conversation, but it finally happens. As soon as I hear the front door click shut I walk into the den, where she is sitting on the couch.

"I need the truth," I say.

She looks up, surprised. "Josie." Then, "Where's Paul?"

"He left. I told him to."

She nods slowly.

"Why did you believe Sully?" I ask.

"What?"

She looks confused, and I realize her mind is on this morning—Officer Sully, not High-School Sully. So I spell it out for her. "After Paul moved away. The Arizona-girlfriend story. Why did you believe Sully?"

My mom frowns. "Why wouldn't I believe Sully? He was Paul's best friend. . . . He'd been in touch with Paul and I hadn't. . . . Why are you asking me this?"

"Paul said there was no girlfriend. Just some girl he was hanging out with, platonically."

My mom shakes her head. "It was more than platonic."

"How do you know?"

"Because I know."

"Did Sully give you any proof?"

"I didn't need *proof*, Josie. Why would he make something like that up?"

"He was hot for you, Paul said."

"Please." My mom snorts. "As soon as the word got out I was pregnant, I was no longer *hot* to anyone. Least of all Sully. It was like I had the plague. No one at school would go near me."

"So what—Sully never talked to you again?"

"Pretty much. Sure, he gave me some bullshit line about how Paul and I should try to work it out for the sake of the baby, but—"

"Why is that a bullshit line?"

"What?"

"Why was Sully telling you to work it out for my sake a *bullshit line*?"

My mother stares at me. "Because. It doesn't change the fact that after I wrote to Paul, telling him I was keeping you,

I never heard from him again. Ever. As you well know."

She sounds remarkably sure about this, but I can't be. There's too much that doesn't add up.

"I *know* about the letters," I say.

"What letters?"

I look straight at her. "The letters Paul sent you from Arizona. . . . I also know how many times he called, and how you refused to talk to him."

She's shaking her head. "He never called."

"Mom. He *told* me."

"Well, he's making it up."

"Why would he do that?"

"I don't know."

"He said you didn't want to see him again after he moved. You didn't want *me* to see him."

She stares at me. "He told you that?"

I nod.

"I don't know why he would tell you that, Josie," she says calmly, but I can see that underneath she's starting to unravel. "He's the one who ended things. *He* broke up with *me*."

"Because he thought you were having an abortion."

She hesitates. "Yes."

"Which you conveniently failed to mention to me until today."

"I know . . . and I'm sorry about that. . . . Josie, I am so very, very —"

"So you're saying Paul never wrote to you after he moved."

She shakes her head. "Not once."

"And he never called."

"No."

"Well." I flop down on the couch next to her. "Someone is lying. That much is clear."

"I agree."

"And you're saying it's not you."

"It's not."

"And Paul says it's not him."

She presses her lips together, silent.

"So I guess the only thing left to do is bust out the Ouija board and have a séance."

"Excuse me?"

"Grandma and Grandpa Gardner. We'll just have to ask them to weigh in from the great beyond." I know I sound ridiculous. But I have to say it.

"What are you *talking* about?" my mom says.

"Paul said your parents didn't like him. Is he lying about that, too?"

She sighs. "They didn't *not like him*. They were . . . protective, that's all. I was their only child."

"So?"

"So, after I told them I was pregnant, they were even more protective. They were . . . well OK, they *were* mad at Paul, for a while. They saw how hurt I was after he moved—after Sully told me what he knew. I was a mess, really. I couldn't sleep . . . refused to eat. And they . . . my mom especially . . ." Her voice trails off.

"What?"

She shakes her head. "Nothing."

I don't let up. *"What?"*

"Nothing. Just . . . she was always saying how I didn't need Paul to raise this baby. I didn't need the Tuccis or their money. She and my dad would take care of everything."

"So, they *didn't* want Paul to talk to you. Or write to you."

"No, they . . ." My mother's face has suddenly gone from pink to white. Her nose is pinched at the corners.

"What?"

She shakes her head. She shakes and shakes like she's trying to physically extricate a thought.

"What?" I say again.

She lets out a shuddering sigh. "It's too crazy."

"Mom. This whole *thing* is crazy."

"I know, but . . ."

"What?"

She shakes her head again.

"Mom."

"OK, it's . . . I need you to come with me, OK?"

"Where?"

"Just humor me, Josie. Can you do that?"

I stare at her. I don't have any clue what she's talking about. But is there any real reason to refuse?

"Fine," I say.

"And grab a sweater," she tells me.

"A sweater," I repeat.

"Two sweaters, OK? One for me."

I nod, start to leave the room, then turn back for a moment. I'm not finished with my questions. Not even close.

But I will wait.

I will go to the hall closet, where we keep our winter clothes, to see what we have for sweaters. And I will put in a call to Liv, telling her to come over, in case my mom is having a nervous breakdown. I just may need the reinforcement.

Fifteen minutes later, my mom and I are in the attic. She was right about the sweaters; it has to be twenty degrees colder up here than in the rest of the house. This is what happens when no one bothers to insulate beyond the pink fluff hanging off the ceiling.

There is also junk everywhere.

Junk, coated in dust.

Unless my grandparents had some sort of bizarre organizational system, it looks like they just dumped stuff every which way. My mother hasn't gone through any of it since they died. At first she thought the process would be too painful. Then she just didn't want to deal with it. And now all these years later, here we are. The most interesting thing I have unearthed so far is one of my grandmother's wigs, which looks just the way I remember it: like a small, dead panther.

"I can't believe she wore these things," my mom says, when I put it in her hands.

"Well," I say, "what would you wear if you were bald?"

"I don't know . . . a kerchief or something."

"I'd wear a baseball hat."

"And *I*," says a voice from the doorway, "would tattoo my entire head. . . . Peace signs, dragonflies—"

"Liv!" I jump up to hug her. I am so glad she's here.

Liv unhooks my arms from her neck. She takes a step forward, staring around the room. "Holy *shite*."

"That's right," my mom says dryly. "Piles and piles of shite."

"Which is why we needed you," I add.

Liv nods. "Clearly."

We've been up here for more than an hour. It's surreal, looking at this stuff—everything my grandparents held on to. Some things I vaguely remember: my grandfather's catcher's mitt, a clock with birds on it, the brown-and-purple afghan that used to lie at the foot of their bed.

My mom tears up a little when I hand it to her. She tells

us about the Christmas she was seven, when she ate an entire bowl of maraschino cherries and threw up on that afghan. She tells us about the games her father used to play with her when she was sick—Tiddlywinks, Blockhead, Spit—and how he would always play left-handed, so she would win.

Now my mom is crouched under the glow of a lamp in one corner of the room, leafing through a stack of papers.

"What's that?" I ask.

"Your great-grandfather's autobiography. Grandpa Gardner's father, my grandfather Julian."

"He wrote an *autobiography*?"

"Apparently."

"Cool!" Liv says, glancing over from the trunk she's been yanking stuff out of and flinging onto the floor. "I want to read it."

"I don't know what I was thinking," my mother says suddenly. "This is ridiculous."

"What is?" I say.

"This!" She gestures wildly around the room. "What we're doing, pulling out all this crap! We're not going to find anything!"

"OK, but . . . what if we did?"

She shakes her head. "I don't know. . . . Maybe it doesn't even matter."

"OK," I say, shrugging. "I'm freezing, anyway."

"Well, let's just do two more boxes. Since we're already up here."

From across the room we hear a huff of breath, then a *holy shite*. Then Liv says softly, "You guys?"

We look over, see the expression on her face.

There is a moment of quiet, an eternity of quiet, as my mom and I get up and walk across the room.

It's an ordinary box. Brown cardboard, unremarkable in every way. But here is Liv, holding it out to my mom. "Katie Gardner?"

And here is my mom, with a gentleness I've only seen her use once in my life—the time we found a hummingbird in the backyard that had flown into our kitchen window and cracked its beak—lifting up an envelope.

Eighteen

I HEAR THE rustling of paper and realize I'm lying in my mother's bed, a stream of sunlight from the window above her dresser hitting me square in the eyes. Using one hand as a visor, I squint at Liv's bobbing head.

"Josie," she whispers. She's holding a sheet of pale blue stationery. "Listen to this."

I scramble to a sitting position. I can feel a trickle of drool in the corner of my mouth. I am still wearing last night's sweater.

"*Dear Katie. Tell me what to do. Tell me what to say. I'll do anything to make this right between us. . . .*

"I know," I tell her. "I read that one."

"OK, but it bears rereading. . . ."

A voice floats up from beneath the covers—my mom's

voice. "Read the one about the horse," she says, peeling a sheet back from her face. Her hair is sticking up at odd angles against the pillow. There's mascara smudged under her eyes. She shed a few tears last night, my mom, reading Paul Tucci's letters. She cried for a while, then something snapped inside her and she hurled the box of letters across the attic, sending paper flying every which way. *How could her parents have done this to her?!* She wanted to know. *Who were they to play God?! Who were they to screw with her life like that, and Paul's life, and mine?!*

I had no idea how to answer her, but Liv did. "I don't think they meant to hurt you, Kate."

"Well, they *did*," my mom said. Then her indignation boiled into fury and she shouted at the roof, "You hear that, assholes?! You hurt me!"

Thinking about it now, I can't believe my mom was mad enough to drop A-bombs on her dead parents. It makes me feel tender toward her this morning—protective. Which is ironic when I think about how we've been treating each other lately. Maybe, in some twisted way, finding these letters was actually a good thing.

"Read the one about the horse," my mom says again.

"What one about the horse?" Liv asks.

I explain. "The one where he threatens to steal his neighbor's horse and gallop across the country to kidnap her if she doesn't write back."

I consider the image of a teenage Paul Tucci on a stallion, baseball hat on backward, Walkman clipped to his ears. It's a ridiculous vision, but Liv nods, as though she can seriously picture it happening. "Boy had it bad for you, Kate," she says.

And my mom says, "I know."

"And *these*..." Liv scrambles across the bed to dig something out of the box. It is the world's tiniest pair of baby socks—white with green frogs. "These kill me."

My mom closes her eyes. "I know."

"I mean, think about it," Liv continues. "He actually walked into a store and picked these out."

Liv tosses the froggy socks to me and I catch them. They are so small. It's crazy to think that these were meant for me—that, once upon a time, my size-9 feet would have fit into them.

"So, what are you going to do, Kate?" Liv asks. "Are you going to call him?"

"I don't know yet," my mom says, shaking her head. "I need to let things . . . marinate for a bit."

"Alternatively . . ." Liv reaches into the box and pulls out a stack of bills. Fives, tens, twenties; a couple of fifties—all money Paul Tucci earned at his summer job as a busboy— all money he tucked into envelopes and sent to my mom. "We could go to Vegas . . ."

"Hey!" I lurch for the money. "That's my diaper fund!"

I know it's not much right now, Paul Tucci wrote. *But it's a start. I know diapers are expensive—*

"Don't worry," Liv says. She cradles the wad of cash to her chest, stroking it gently. "I'll give this baby a good home. A *very* good home."

My mom snorts.

"You are such a freak," I say.

"It's called *humor,* people. And it's very therapeutic. You should try it sometime."

We make it to school, barely. Riggs is waiting at my locker, just as I'd imagined he would be. When I see him, my stomach sinks and my heart jumps at the same time. The expression on his face isn't exactly what I'd expected. He doesn't look worried; he looks pissed. "Where have you been?" he says. "Why haven't you answered my voice mails?"

I wasn't prepared for anger, and I'm not sure how to respond. Am I supposed to apologize? Cry? He's the one who was acting like a sex-crazed jerk the other night.

Luckily Liv launches in, full throttle. "So Josie calls me, and she's like, 'Liv, come over. We're up in the attic, searching for Tucci letters.' So I drive over there, and she and her mom are both just rooting around through all of her grandparents' old, dust-encrusted crap—"

"Paul insisted he wrote these letters," I interrupt, "but my mom kept telling me, 'Josie, he's making it up.' Then, the minute I brought up my grandmother's name, she was like—"

"Her own parents intercepted her mail! They never even *opened* anything, they just shoved it all in a box and hid it."

"Seriously?" Riggs asks. He's staring from Liv to me with those bluest of blue eyes.

I nod. "It's not how it sounds, though. They were trying to protect her."

The second bell rings and Liv gives me a quick hug before sprinting to her locker so she won't be late for class. All around us, bodies are moving, doors are slamming, but Riggs is still standing here, looking into my eyes.

"That's unbelievable," he says.

And I say, "I know."

"So, what now?"

I shake my head. "No clue."

Here we are looking at each other and, before I know it, Riggs leans in so close I can smell his toothpaste. "About the other night . . . I was an asshole."

I pull back, look him in the eye again. "Yes. You were."

"I'm sorry," he says, bending in to kiss me.

But I pull back again. "This is huge for me, Matt, my father being back. Huge. And sometimes I'm going to want to talk about it. Not just hook up. *Talk*. And you're going to have to listen."

Riggs nods. "I know."

"Well . . . good."

"I'm sorry."

"OK."

He hesitates, then asks, "Can I kiss you now?"

I am about to say yes, but Mr. Charney, the hall monitor, has waddled up to us with his clipboard. If we don't get to class in the next three seconds, he threatens, we'll have detention.

Riggs and I squeeze hands. We hold on as long as we can. Then we force ourselves to walk in opposite directions.

The whole day is weird. One moment my brain is perfectly functional, solving quadratic equations, the next I am picturing Paul Tucci's letters. Piles of them. Line after line of his tiny block print. There's one in particular I can't get out of my head—not a letter, but a card. On the front are two green birds against a blue sky. The first bird is saying, "I love you more," and the second one is saying, "No. I love you more." Inside it says, "Let this be our only disagreement." I must have read that card a dozen times last night. Enough to remember what he wrote.

> *Dear Katie,*
>
>   *I miss you so much I can't describe it. Today when I got home from school I tried working on this essay I've been procrastinating over, but you*

have this power over me that won't let me think
about anything else. I don't mind the feeling
though. I love you. Please tell me that even
though I haven't heard from you you're having
as much trouble concentrating as I am, because
then maybe I won't feel like such a jackass. You
don't know how much I want to see you again.
You AND the baby. I love you both.

—PAUL

You AND the baby. I love you both.

All day long, those words are bouncing around the back of my skull, like tiny rubber balls. It's a wonder my head doesn't fly off.

While Liv and I are getting dressed for practice, Coach sends one of the JV girls into the locker room to get us. A ponytailed head pokes through the doorway. "Josie and Olivia? . . . Coach wants to see you in his office."

Office is the generous term for the old janitor's closet off the boys' locker room. When Liv and I get there, Coach pushes the door shut. His EHS Hurricanes sweatshirt and matching polyester shorts have been starched into submission, and the whistle around his neck gleams in the fluorescent light.

"Sit," Coach says, leaning back in his chair, tapping his fingertips together.

Liv and I glance at each other. We know it's bad. We slump onto the metal stools that have been set up for us, and we wait.

"So . . ." Coach says. "The two of you missed practice yesterday. Strange, since a little birdie tells me she saw you both in the locker room five minutes before."

What kind of birdie? That's my question. *A Jamie birdie or a Schuyler birdie? Surely not a Kara birdie. A Kara birdie would never—*

"Apparently," Coach continues, "you had somewhere more important to go. . . . Would anyone care to elaborate? . . . Josie?"

The office smells like soccer socks and pine cleaner. I don't know what to tell Coach. *I have no clue what you're talking about? I was dragged out of the school building against my will by my delinquent but well-intentioned best friend?* Or how about the truth?

Here is the truth: I don't know what the truth is anymore. Three months ago, I couldn't have imagined feeling this way. Three months ago, I trusted my mother's word and Paul Tucci was just a figment of my imagination. Three months ago . . .

Coach is tapping his fingertips, blinking at me.

"Yes," I tell him. "We skipped practice."

I look over at Liv, who is nodding.

"And we take full responsibility for our actions."

Coach lowers his hands to his desk and clears his throat.

"In that case, I have no choice but to suspend you for the next three games."

"*Three games?*" Liv's jaw is on the floor.

"Are you serious?" I say.

It's already the end of October. Three games means East Hampton, Cathedral, Greenfield. . . . It means the difference between play-offs and no play-offs. Three games could mean the season.

"You choose to disrespect your teammates?" Coach says. "You choose to think that the rules of this team don't apply to you? You choose to suffer the penalty."

We're still in shock when he glances down at his watch. "Well," he says, pushing down on his desk and rising slowly, "time for practice."

Liv and I glance at each other.

"Um . . ." I say.

And Liv says, "Do we still come to practice?"

"Of course." Now Coach is smiling. "I would *never* deny a player the privilege of practice."

Here is what "practice" is when you have chosen to disregard Coach's rules: "Practice" is running wind sprints until your legs are Jell-O and you're dry-heaving facedown in the dirt. "Practice" is one hundred squat thrusts followed by one hundred push-ups followed by enough stomach crunches to make even Arnold Schwarzenegger weep. "Practice" is enduring the venomous stare-downs of your teammates for two hours straight.

"Sorry about that," Liv says as we're limping back toward the locker room, alone, because everyone is too mad to talk to us.

With what little strength I have left, I smack her in the butt. "You'd better be."

Nineteen

THE NEXT AFTERNOON, Liv and I sit on the bench in our home uniforms, watching our team get creamed by Cathedral High School.

"This is beyond punishment," she mutters. "This is torture."

"Brutal," I agree.

At first I thought that not being able to play was the worst possible thing—second to the fact that right now we are losing six to one. Third to the fact that our teammates have yet to forgive us for our trespasses.

But I realize I'm wrong.

The worst part is that my mom is alone in the bleachers.

Seeing her sitting there, blowing into her hands to stay warm, I feel a wave of sadness come over me. *Sadness*, of all things. Here she is, without Jonathan, focused exclusively on me—just what I wanted, right?

Well, as it turns out, no. This morning, before Liv and I left for school, I walked into my mom's bedroom to say good-bye and she was still lying in bed, staring at the ceiling. I sat down next to her, and she said, "Jonathan and I are taking a break." I didn't say anything, just looked at her. "It was my decision," she said.

"Is it because of—" I started to ask.

But she cut me off. "This has nothing to do with Paul. . . . Or, well, it has very little to do with Paul. . . . Mostly, it has to do with how fast everything's been happening."

"It has been fast," I agreed.

"And how *needy* Jonathan is. He wants . . . a lot from me, emotionally. . . . At first it was flattering, but . . . well, I'm not sure I'm ready to give it to him. . . . So we're taking some time apart. To think things through."

"Oh," I said. "Uh-huh." Then, "OK."

I let her think I was glad about it. The truth is, though, I was a little shocked. I thought she was into him. And I can say for a fact—based on Jonathan's and my Virtual Boogie/Slurpee excursion yesterday—that he's still into her.

I don't really get how "taking a break" is any different from "breaking up," but one thing I do know: I don't like seeing my mom sitting alone in the bleachers.

*   *   *

In the car after the game, she says, "Do you want to tell me why you didn't play today?"

"Not really," I say.

"Are you hurt?"

I shake my head.

"Josie. . . . Are you in trouble?"

I hesitate. Then say, "You won't like it."

"I'll like it a lot less if you don't tell me."

So I do. I tell her what happened yesterday, about blowing off practice, about Coach suspending us.

And then, once the confession gates have opened, I tell her about Liv.

My mom's eyes never leave my face. I watch her mouth open as she takes a breath. "Liv thought she was pregnant?"

"Yes," I say. Then, "But you can't *say* anything to her, Mom. I'm sure she'll tell you herself at some point, but—"

"I won't."

"I'm only telling you because it's . . . relevant."

She raises her eyebrows.

"You and Paul. The whole mess . . . Liv thinks I can't understand what you went through because I haven't been there."

My mom nods. "Ah."

"But maybe I *can* understand, sort of. The way things are with me and Matt . . . maybe I *do* get it—"

"Wait," she says. "Back up. The last I heard about you and Matt was the kiss at the party . . . and something about a cheerleader . . ."

"Oh my God," I say. "You are so behind."

"Well . . . catch me up."

So I do. I tell her all about dinner at Matt's house and meeting his family and how we can talk on the phone for hours. I tell her about the fight we had the other night and how good it felt to make up this morning. I tell her that I've never felt this way before, about anyone, ever.

My mom nods, smiling a little. "I'm happy for you." Then her face gets serious. "Josie. If the two of you are . . ."

"We're not."

"If you're having—"

"We're not having sex, Mom. We're taking it slow."

She breathes out, a long, steady stream. "OK. . . . But if you ever decide—"

I hold up my hand to stop her. "I know. Condoms. Spermicide. The Pill. The diaphragm. The cervical cap. . . ."

She nods, nods, nods.

"I'm not a complete idiot, OK?"

The minute the words come out of my mouth I'm sorry. My regret makes me want to puke.

"Mom. I didn't mean . . ."

"I know," she says quietly. There's a long pause, and then, "I never told anyone this before, but I'm going to tell you now." She glances over at me, and her face is wide open, in a way I've never seen before. "OK?"

I nod. I want her to tell me. I *need* her to.

"I changed my mind on the bus, on my way to the clinic.

I was by myself because Paul had already moved . . . and, well, he wouldn't have gone with me anyway. He'd made that clear. And I . . . couldn't bring myself to tell my parents yet.

"Anyway, the bus stopped and this woman got on. She was wearing one of those baby-carrier thingies. I forget what they're called . . . it doesn't matter. . . . She sat down next to me and she, you know, peeled back the cloth to lift the baby out. At first, I couldn't look at it. I made myself look away, out the window, at the backpack in my lap, anywhere but at that baby. But then the mom turns to me and she says, 'I think he likes you.' So I looked. I looked at that baby and he was just . . . gazing up at me, with one of those gummy little grins. And . . . I don't know what happened. The kid wasn't even cute. He had a huge head. And a ridiculous amount of hair, parted on the side. He looked like a miniature investment banker. Like Donald Trump. But I swear to God, Josie, I changed my mind right there. In that instant."

"You decided to keep me."

"I decided to keep you."

"Even though I might have come out looking like Donald Trump."

"Even then."

"Huh," I say. I smile a little, picturing myself with a strawberry-blonde comb-over. Would Riggs still go out with me?

My mom continues, her voice calm and quiet. Her hands

are clasped in her lap. "When I got home I did two things. I wrote to Paul to tell him I was keeping the baby, and I told my parents I was pregnant. . . . They were pretty shocked, obviously. My mom cried. My dad . . . he was a bit more pragmatic. He wanted to know if I'd seen an obstetrician yet. If I'd started taking vitamins . . . prenatals, you know, to keep the baby healthy. He wanted me to think about adoption. . . ."

I raise my eyebrows.

My mom looks straight at me. "I told him no way. I said I was keeping this baby, no matter what. Whatever it took, I was keeping you."

I nod, swallowing the lump that has suddenly appeared at the base of my throat.

She hesitates, then keeps going. "That was before Sully told me what he told me. He didn't just say Paul had a new girlfriend, Josie. He gave *specifics*. Like how gorgeous she was. Things they'd done together. How crazy Paul was about her. . . . And I believed him. Maybe I shouldn't have, but I did. I thought about sending Paul another letter, but every time I sat down to write it, I'd remind myself that he hadn't written me back after the first one. He hadn't called. Why should I put myself out there again? There was a pride thing . . . and a devastation thing. You can't imagine how devastated I was."

Yes, I can, I think. *If Riggs ever did that to me . . .*

"I could barely get out of bed in the morning. . . . My

parents . . . well, they just took over. . . . They pulled me out of school . . . bought the house in Elmherst. They wanted me to have a fresh start, after you were born. A clean slate. They weren't . . ." She hesitates, staring down at her hands, which are still clutched in her lap. "I couldn't sleep last night, thinking about what they did, keeping Paul away from me, and . . . I don't think they were bad people for doing it. They didn't want me to get hurt, any more than I already was. They did everything they could to ensure that."

There's a catch in my mom's voice, and for a second I think she might cry, but then she turns to me and says, almost fiercely, "And I would do the same thing for you. Whatever it took."

"Steal my boyfriend's letters?" I ask wryly.

She shakes her head. "No—"

"I'm kidding, Mom. I know what you're saying."

"Do you?"

"Yes."

She sighs. "Good."

We sit in silence for a minute. Then she says quietly, "I didn't mean for things to end up this way, Josie."

"I know."

"There's so much I could have done differently. . . . Things I *should* have done differently. For you. Like trying to find Paul—"

"Mom. It's OK."

"No." She shakes her head. "I was scared. And . . . selfish. I didn't want . . . every time I thought about finding him, or him finding us . . . I was afraid that if he came back into our life . . ."

"What?"

"I might lose you."

I can't believe what I'm hearing—like I would ever, in a million years, choose Paul Tucci over her. I think about Mel's parents, and Schuyler's—how ever since they split up they've been fighting over who gets to keep the kids. But that's different. That's divorce.

"Mom," I say. "Come on."

She shakes her head. "You don't understand. Paul's family had money. After your grandparents died, I was just . . . a single mom with a GED, working in a bookstore. The Tuccis could have . . . if they'd gotten a lawyer . . . I just couldn't risk losing you."

"I know."

"I'm sorry."

"I know, Mom," I say. Then, "I'm sorry too."

"What? This isn't your fault. You didn't have anything to do with—"

"Not about Paul. Just . . . I know I've been kind of a jerk to you lately. And Jonathan . . . But I *did* try to redeem myself yesterday. I took him to the Pizza Palace to play video games."

"You did?" She looks surprised.

"*And* I bought him a Slurpee. His first Slurpee ever, I might add. . . . It really helped to assuage my guilt."

Now she smiles. "I was hoping the guilt gene would skip a generation."

"No such luck."

"Well," she says. "I'm sorry about that, too."

She starts to say something else, then changes her mind and turns the key in the ignition, revving the engine.

It is the quietest drive, after all that talking. The strangest, quietest thing. My mom and I don't even turn on the radio. We just drive home together, side by side, thought bubbles floating over both our heads.

Twenty

SUNDAY NIGHT, AND my mom and I are sitting on the couch in the Weiss-Longos' living room. I am eating cocktail peanuts while she fidgets.

"Relax," I tell her. I gesture to the wineglass on the coffee table. "Have some Merlot." Instead, she taps her foot against the hardwood floor and stares down at her fingernails, which Liv has painted the color of smoked salmon. "Orange means vitality, Kate," is what she said, "and balance."

If there's anything my mother could use right now, it's balance.

"Everything's going to be fine," I tell her, holding the glass out to her until she takes a sip. "Don't worry."

It was Liv's idea to invite Paul Tucci for dinner. She got Pops and Dodd on board right away. I thought my mother would flat-out refuse, but she surprised us all by saying yes. She wouldn't let Dodd do her hair, though. And she insisted on wearing her rattiest sweatshirt—the two-toned one with the paint splatters and the holes in the elbows—which I couldn't believe.

"Don't you want to look *halfway* decent?" I asked her, when she walked out of her bedroom.

"This isn't about impressing anyone, Josie," she said.

And I said, "Well, what is it about then?"

She shook her head, struggling to come up with an answer. "I don't know. Putting it out there. . . . Moving on. . . ."

"Anyway," I say now, "you've already seen each other twice. I don't get what you're so nervous about."

But I do get it.

Tonight is different.

She found his letters, and she read them, and now, everything she thought she knew has been flipped on its head.

I'm a little nervous myself. I don't know how things will go tonight. It could be a disaster. But at least we'll have Liv and Pops and Dodd and Wyatt here with us—the Weiss-Longo buffer zone. If the poop hits the fan, I guarantee one of them will find a way to distract from the splatter. Liv's outfit alone could do that job.

Here she is, standing in the doorway, holding a tray of cheese. Ruffly black chambermaid's dress with apron; chef's hat; towel, folded over one arm.

"*Bonsoir, mesdemoiselles,*" she says, sweeping her way across the living room. "*Apéritif?*"

"I don't think I can eat," my mom says. Panic lines erupt on her brow. "I might barf," she adds.

Right on cue, Pops arrives in the doorway to announce that the pork tenderloin is sizzling, the potatoes have been whipped, and all is well with the universe. He gazes fondly across the room at my mom. "Are we drinking our wine, Kate?"

"Not really," I tell him. "I keep trying to make her."

"You need to relax," Pops says.

"I realize that," my mother says, "but everyone *telling* me to relax doesn't *make* me relax. It makes me the *opposite* of relax."

"OK," Pops says soothingly. He walks over to join her on the couch, pats her knee. "OK."

A second later, the doorbell chimes.

Nobody moves.

"Hon?" Dodd calls from the kitchen. "Would you get that? My hands are covered in dressing!"

Pops starts to rise, but my mom beats him to it. "Let me do this," she says, standing. "I should be the one to do this."

It is her voice that surprises me, the strength of it.

"You *go*, girl," Liv mumbles through a mouthful of cheese.

We watch my mom cross the room, her back straight. This is huge for her, this moment.

How can we not follow?

Standing on the porch, Paul Tucci looks more like Paul Bunyan: plaid flannel shirt tucked into jeans, hiking boots. Only this time he's not wearing a baseball cap, so I can actually see his hair—wavy on top, a single curl flopping onto his forehead like a question mark.

He holds out a hand to my mom, as though they're meeting for the first time. "Hello, Katie."

"Paul." Whatever she's feeling inside, she sounds calm. I, on the other hand, am a bundle of nerves.

"I come bearing pesto," Paul Tucci says, holding out a jar.

"*Pesto,*" Pops whispers in my ear. I can tell he's impressed.

Thanks to her bionic hearing, my mom whips around and narrows her eyes at us, like she's not amused that we're hiding behind the coatrack.

Pops takes the hint. "You must be Paul," he says, stepping out into the open. "I'm Gregory."

The two of them shake hands. Then Paul looks over Pops's shoulder, meeting my eye-line. "Hi, Josie." His smile is slow, tentative.

"Hi," I say back, just as cautious. And then something hits me. It is easier this time, seeing him. Easier than it was at the hospital, easier than the night on my porch. This time, I know something I didn't before. I know Paul Tucci isn't a liar.

For dinner, Liv made place cards for everyone—little tents of white paper with our names on them. Surprise, surprise, she put Paul in the middle, between me and my mom. As an added bonus, she put herself directly across from him—Dr. Steve, ready for her interview.

As soon as we sit down, I shoot her a look: *Keep your mouth shut.*

Liv widens her eyes: *Who, me?* She asks Paul to pass the salt and pepper, which he does.

He has long fingers. I notice that one of his fingernails is black and wonder what he was doing when he banged it. That happened to me once in seventh grade, in shop. The hammer slipped while I was trying to build a birdhouse.

"This is fantastic," Paul says, meaning the food.

"Dodd's a regular Rachael Ray," Liv says.

Dodd smiles serenely. "I prefer Julia Child."

Wyatt hums while he eats; he always has. When he asks for something to be passed to him, he uses his own lingo. "Gravity" for gravy. "Roulders" for rolls. We're used to it, but you have to wonder what Paul Tucci is thinking. He had a laugh-smile on his face when Wyatt asked him to pass the "stinky little cabbages," but maybe he was just being polite.

We're all being polite. Chewing with our mouths closed. Making small talk. No one swears or burps. Everyone says please. It's unnerving.

"More Merlot anyone?" Pops asks, holding up the bottle.

"Yes, please," my mom and Paul Tucci answer together. They have both been sipping wine at an impressive pace. I don't think I've ever seen my mom have more than one drink at dinner. She's a lightweight. I'm nervous for her, afraid of what might fly out of her mouth at any second. Meanwhile, Paul Tucci's cheeks have taken on the flushed, feverish look that I have seen on many a high-school boy's face at many a high-school party.

I consider the image of a teenage Katie Gardner and Paul Tucci packed into someone's basement rec room on a Friday night, plastic cups in hand, yelling to hear each other over the pounding of the boom box.

I catch Liv's eye across the table. Liv, who, other than using a French accent, has shown a surprising level of restraint during this meal.

Awkward, I mouth to her.

She raises her eyebrows delicately.

Say something! I want to shout.

But someone else reads my mind. "Hey," Paul Tucci's voice blurts out beside me, "is that my sweatshirt?"

I turn to see my mother shaking her head. "No. It's mine."

"I know it's *yours*," he says. "I mean, I gave it to you." He looks around the table at all of us. "I gave her that sweatshirt," he explains, "for her birthday."

Wyatt laughs. "Rough."

"Forgive our son," Pops says. "He's missing the sentimentality gene."

"Well, I love it," Liv says, squinting discerningly across the table. "*Très* nineties, no?"

I lean forward to get a good look at my mom's face, which is pink. *Now* I know why she wore a crusty, moth-eaten sweat rag to dinner. She wasn't so much rebelling as testing. *Paul Tucci passes!*

"I can't believe you still have it," he says, staring at her.

"Yeah, well . . . I can't believe you remember."

A long pause and then Dodd says, "Why don't you two . . . go into the den to catch up? We'll make coffee." He looks pointedly at Pops and Wyatt and Liv and me, as if it takes a village to make a pot of Folgers.

So my mom and Paul have gone into the den, to talk. Or to drink more wine. Or to do whatever it is they need to do.

It feels weirdly right—fitting—that this is happening in the Weiss-Longos' house. It's our house too, in a way. My mom and I have so much history here: the time Liv and I rode down the stairs in a sleeping bag and both ended up splitting our chins open, getting stitches; the time my mom made a birthday cake for Pops and set the oven on fire. We've shared a thousand meals, a million stories, laughs, occasional tears—like the summer Dodd's mother died and we all took the road trip to Florida, and the hotel we stayed in had cockroaches the size of golf balls.

I am reminded, sitting in this kitchen, that this is my family. Maybe we don't share the same blood, but who cares? That's what we are.

I am sitting on my favorite bar stool—the one with the rip in the seat. Liv is beside me.

"Well," she says, looking at her watch. "It's been fourteen minutes."

"Fourteen minutes," I repeat.

"It's good they're talking."

"Yes."

"So you've got yourself a dad, huh, Josie?" Wyatt asks from his perch on the counter, where he is trying to crack walnuts with a pair of spaghetti tongs.

"I don't know about that, Wy. Let's see if he sends a Christmas card before we start handing out titles."

I am kidding, but not. I don't think I could ever call Paul Tucci "Dad." It would feel fake. A dad is someone who held you on the day you were born—who has never missed a birthday, or a soccer game, or a parent-teacher conference. Besides, I don't know what it means yet, him being here. I don't know if it changes anything. I don't know if I want it to.

"Coffee's ready," Dodd says, holding up the pot. "And

I made cheesecake, and brownies. Oh, and there's Häagen-Dazs. Three different kinds. . . . I wasn't sure, you know . . ." he turns to me, "what Paul would like."

"Right." I smile weakly, realizing that we are all thinking the same thing: Who is this guy, really?

"Don't worry," Pops says sweetly to Dodd, leaning over to smooch his cheek. "Everyone loves your cheesecake."

Wyatt makes a gagging sound—it's unclear whether it's the cheesecake or the kissing that offends, but either way no one calls him on it because now my mom is standing in the doorway.

"Josie?"

Her face looks calm, but rosy, like she's just gotten back from a run. Sometimes I forget how pretty she is. Long, dark eyelashes. High, delicate cheekbones with just a smattering of freckles. I see her face every day, but I don't really notice it, the same way I don't really notice the wallpaper in my bedroom. Meanwhile, here she is, beautiful.

"Yeah?" I say.

She wants me to come into the den with her and Paul, to talk. Suddenly my stomach is flipping all over the place. *Talk?* About what? What do they expect me to say? We're supposed to be eating cheesecake!

"OK," I tell my mom. Then, "I'll meet you in there, though. I have to go pee first."

"Go pee," she says. "We'll meet you in there."

✳   ✳   ✳

I don't really need to pee. What I need to do is stare at myself in the bathroom mirror for a while, to see if I'm ready, if I can deal. Staring back at me is a girl with big brown eyes and a ponytail that's half falling out of its elastic. She looks a little freaked. Not a lot, but a little.

I have this fantasy, while I'm standing in the bathroom—a fantasy I've never allowed myself to have before. I will walk into the den and my mom and Paul Tucci will be sitting on the Weiss-Longos' couch, holding hands. They will see me in the doorway, and they will smile. They won't have to say a word because I will know. They have never stopped loving each other. They are getting back together.

"You're an idiot," the girl in the mirror says to me. Or I say to her. Either way, it's true.

Of *course* I don't expect my mom and Paul Tucci to get back together. That would be ludicrous. Asinine. But I can't help the image; it just pops in there. It's because, when you've spent sixteen years without something, and that something suddenly appears, you don't know what to think. You have no way to process it. All you can do is stare at yourself in the mirror until you are ready to leave the bathroom.

Am I ready?

No.

But somehow my feet are moving.

Walking down the hall, I picture another gem of a scenario. I picture Paul Tucci on the couch next to my mom.

"Katie, please," he's saying. "Let me buy you and Josie a beach house on the Carolina coast."

"No," my mom says, shaking her head and frowning.

"It's the least I can do," he says, "after all you've been through."

"It's not your fault."

"But I feel responsible."

"You shouldn't."

"Maybe not," he says. "But I do."

"OK," my mom says. "You can buy us a beach house.

"Great," Paul Tucci says.

"And we'd like a ski condo too. Josie's never been skiing."

"Of course. She's my daughter. She can have whatever she wants."

Am I an idiot? I am such an idiot.

In the real den, not the den in my mind, they are sitting in separate chairs. When I walk in they are gasping for air, like something hysterical just happened and they can't stop laughing. Which throws me.

"What's so funny?" I ask.

"Josie," Paul Tucci says, pulling himself together right away. "Hi."

I stare at my mom, who is still giggling. I say, "Are you drunk?"

She shakes her head, unable to answer.

"Just reminiscing," Paul explains. "High-school stories."

"Oh," I say.

I take a seat on the couch, across from them.

My mom gives one last shuddering snort, then smiles.

"You should really lay off the booze," I tell her.

"Honey," she says, ignoring my comment. "I'm glad you're here."

"Why?"

She looks at Paul, who clears his throat and looks at me.

I'm about to blurt out that it's time for dessert—Dodd's world-famous cheesecake—but I don't. I realize I want to hear what he has to say.

"Josie." Paul's brown eyes are on mine.

"Uh-huh." My mouth is a cotton ball. I know this is where the big pronouncement comes in, but I have no clue what it will be.

Paul takes a deep breath. "I want to be here," he says.

When I speak, my voice is so low I can barely hear it. "What do you mean?"

"I mean . . . in whatever capacity you want me to be"—he hesitates—"a presence, in your life, I will be. From now on."

I shake my head. I'm not saying *no*, I'm just trying to understand. "Do you mean moving back here?"

"That's a possibility," he says, "at some point."

I can't speak, so I nod.

"I'm committed to my job until the end of the school year. But it's only a two-hour plane ride from Raleigh-Durham . . . and we can talk on the phone, and e-mail. . . . And if you want, at some point . . . I'd like for you to meet Lauren. . . ."

"Lauren," I repeat.

"My fiancée."

It takes me a beat to remember—Big Nick told Liv that Paul had a girlfriend, and Liv told me. But apparently we never got the engagement memo. And now it feels like a bucket of ice water has been dumped on my head.

"Right," I say.

I turn to my mom, to see how she's taking it. Her face is smooth and she's nodding, like she already got the news. And for some unfathomable reason, she's OK with it.

"Lauren's great," Paul Tucci says. "She teaches first grade," he adds, as though this proves her greatness.

I nod again, not knowing what to say. Then something comes to me. "I hated my first-grade teacher."

Paul laughs.

"I did! Remember her, Mom? Mrs. Butterfield? She was mean. And she smelled like Limburger cheese."

"Limburger cheese?" my mom says. "Did you even know what Limburger cheese was when you were six?"

"I love Limburger," Paul says. "All the stinky cheeses, in fact. Camembert. Stilton. The stinkier the better."

Something hits me. We don't know each other at all. I swallow, look down at my lap.

"Josie?" he says.

I shake my head.

"What is it?" my mom says.

"Nothing. Just . . . this is so weird. How do we do it? Where do we start? You know?"

"Well," my mom says slowly. She looks at Paul, and then she looks at me. "I think you already did."

I know what she's doing. She's trying to sound all supportive and encouraging. She wants to prove that she's fine with everything. Fine with Lauren. Fine with me and Paul Tucci suddenly starting this . . . *relationship* . . . when he hasn't been here for the past sixteen years. He's missed my whole life. How can she be OK with that?

"Whatever," I mutter.

I hear how snotty my voice sounds, and it's not how I mean it. I mean that she doesn't have to pretend; she should just admit how she's feeling.

Maybe Paul Tucci can read minds, or maybe he wants to put things in perspective. Either way, he reaches out to punch my mom's shoulder—lightly, like a brother—then turns to me. "We just . . . muddle our way through it."

I understand now—he means all of us. We'll muddle our way through it together.

I start to make a crack about him and Lauren, my mom

and Jonathan on a double date, but then I remember my mom and Jonathan are on a break. Anyway, Paul's face is serious. He's looking for a real response, not a joke. So I tell him I wish he hadn't missed the last sixteen years.

"Me too," he says, and his voice sounds a little choked. "But I'd like to be here for the next sixteen. And the sixteen after that."

I pause to do the math. "I'll be forty-eight," I say. "And you guys will be . . . sixty-four. *God*."

My mom shakes her head, as though she can't imagine herself old.

Neither can I.

Suddenly I want to see my whole future. I'd like to deal out some of those tarot cards and see the three of us, thirty-two years from now. How many marriages will there be? How many children? Will we all be in the same place for Christmas?

Everything I'm imagining is hopeful, but then I worry I'm deluding myself. I want to believe what Paul is saying— about being here—but I'm scared he'll change his mind. No matter what, I will take my mom's side. She's been here from Day 1. And she has never left.

"Josie?" my mom says now. "Are you OK?"

I nod.

"Are you sure? You look—"

"I'm just thinking."

"About . . . ?"

I shake my head, trying to come up with an answer. When I finally say, "Cheesecake," Paul laughs.

"Cheesecake?"

"Yeah," I say. Then, "How do you feel about cheesecake? Do you like it, or is it not stinky enough for you?"

"I love cheesecake," he says.

So I gesture toward the doorway. "Dodd's cheesecake is out there . . . you know, waiting for us."

Paul says, "I hate to leave a cheesecake in the lurch. . . ."

I take this as my cue to stand. Also as my cue to hold out a hand to my mom, to pull her up. So the three of us can walk out together.

Twenty-one

TEN DAYS LATER, Paul Tucci calls from North Carolina. He's back at work, zip-lining through the woods with juvenile delinquents, but soon he'll be on winter break, and he already bought his plane ticket. He'll stay with his parents, so he can keep an eye on Big Nick—make sure he lays off the eggnog. If there's snow, he says, he wants to teach me to ski.

I thought it would be awkward, talking to him on the phone. But it happens not to be so bad. The weird thing is when he asks to talk to my mom, or when she asks to talk to him. Listening to the two of them converse is like walking straight into the Twilight Zone. I sit here, thinking, *My parents are talking on the phone. My parents are talking on the phone!*

The novelty still hasn't worn off. I blab about it to anyone who will listen: Liv, Riggs, even the Makeup Mafia, who, after a week of intense shunning, finally forgave me and Liv for our suspensions. It helps that they lost only one of their three games without us. It also helps that we finally told them what happened—that we didn't ditch practice just to ditch; there was some legitimate drama behind it. I'd forgotten how much Jamie and Lindsey and Schuyler love the drama.

Liv hasn't told them about Finn, though. She is still nursing a sore heart, is my theory. Or at least a bruised ego. I know she says it was all physical between her and Finn—no strings attached—but still. I keep trying to make her laugh with my dumb jokes, and I've put Riggs on the case, to help find a new and improved boy toy—an *anti*-boy toy—which Liv may not be ready for. But she deserves it.

Also still trying is Jonathan, who, while he hasn't materialized on our front porch again, has been calling my mom constantly. I am starting to understand what she meant by the word "needy." At first when he called, it was sweet. She would get off the phone and say, "It was sweet of him to check in." And I would say, "Yes, it was." But then, like an hour later, he would call again. And an hour after that. And an hour after that.

Now I am thinking, *needy* doesn't gel with Kate Gardner. It's not that Jonathan is a bad guy; he's not. . . . It's just, here is the thing: Kate Gardner is a strong, smart, incredible, beautiful person. Kate Gardner deserves someone who's not only nuts about her—who not only holds his arms open wide, with no pretense, no bull—but can stand on his own two feet, watching her do her thing.

This hits me when I swing by the bookstore on Saturday, and my mom is running story hour. She is reading *Mike Mulligan and His Steam Shovel,* and I see the kids sitting cross-legged on the floor, staring up at her, their little mouths gaping open. She isn't just reading; she's doing different voices for all the characters; she's making engine noises; she's standing on her chair, peering down into an imaginary cellar, calling, "Hey, Mike Mulligan, how are you going to get out?!"

I forget, for a second, that she is my mother. And then I remember. And my heart squeezes in on itself, proud.

Later, when we get home, there's bouquet of roses waiting for my mom on the porch. Shocker: They're from Jonathan. Now I have to ask, "So what's the deal with you guys?"

Again, she gives me the party line: they're taking some time apart, time to think things through, time to let things marinate.

"How *much* time?" I ask. I sound exasperated, even to myself. "Just what are you waiting for, exactly? If you think he's too needy, why don't you break up with him for good?"

While she thinks, I hold on to my biggest point: I hope she's not waiting for a Paul Tucci miracle.

"I guess," my mom says finally, "I want to be sure that

whatever I decide about Jonathan, I'm doing it for the right reasons."

"You mean not just because Paul's getting married."

I can't believe I've said it. But it's what I've been thinking for the past week—ever since Paul informed us that Lauren will be coming with him for Christmas.

My mom shakes her head slowly. "More that I don't want to stay with Jonathan just to avoid being alone."

"Mom. You're not *alone*."

"Oh, I know. But next year you'll be a senior. You'll be applying to colleges, and then . . ." She looks at me, shrug-smiles. "You'll be off."

"Well, not permanently!" I say. "And who knows, maybe I'll go to UMass. Or Elmherst College. Maybe I'll only be five minutes away and we'll still see each other, like, all the time."

"Oh, honey." She sighs. "I don't want that."

"Why not? If you need me to—"

"No. It's *my* job, Josie, to sort out my life. Not yours. Your job is to hang out with your friends and have fun and play soccer and . . . you know . . . be young. I haven't let you do enough of that."

"Yes, you have."

"I want you to do it *more*, though, is the point. . . . I want you to really cherish this time. OK? I want you to live it up."

"OK," I say, shrugging. "Great." I tell her I'll be all over it:

keg stands, drag racing, ditching school to shoplift at the mall.

Even though she knows I'm kidding, she pinches my thigh. And even though I know there's no one here to save me, I squeal for help.

Because that is what we do.

I am at Fiorello's, standing at the coffee bar, restocking plastic lids. Bob is behind me, hovering. Ever since the thing with Big Nick, Bob has been hovering. My first day back, when he asked for a Big Nick report, I told him everything I knew— including that minor tidbit I'd left out from the beginning. "By the way . . . did I mention he's my grandfather?"

At this, Bob practically fell over from shock. So of course I had to tell him the whole story.

"It's true," I said, when I'd finished. "You saved my grandfather's life."

Now, whenever I bring it up—the enormity of what he did—Bob brushes it away, embarrassed. But secretly, I know he's pleased. He keeps the bouquet of lilies from the Tuccis smack in the middle of the pastry counter, where everyone can see them, and he hasn't even bothered cleaning up the petals that have started to fall off. The card is cream-colored with a green leaf border and a single line of script:

> *Yours forever in gratitude, Nico, Christina,*
> *Peter, Patrick, and Paul Tucci.*

While I restock, I think about the night before Paul left for North Carolina, how he brought his parents by my house, and we all sat around the kitchen table. It was the first time my mom and I had seen them since the hospital—the first time since Paul told them about me.

It could have been horrendously, torturously awkward, and, in a way, it was. One thing about Christina Tucci: she doesn't mince words. She thinks Paul and my mom screwed up royally, and she wasn't afraid to say it. She thinks she and Big Nick were robbed of the opportunity to be my grandparents, and she wasn't afraid to say that, either. In a way, my impression of her hasn't changed since that first night at Shop-Co, when she badgered the checkout girl and slapped her husband on the wrist for picking up a Peppermint Pattie. But I think I might admire her too, a little. For speaking her mind. For putting her feelings out there.

And anyway, Big Nick's humor is the perfect antidote for Christina's crustiness. Like how, in the middle of her tirade, he winked across the kitchen table at me and said loudly, "You can be glad of one thing, Josie. You didn't get the Tucci nose."

"What's wrong with the Tucci nose?" Christina said. Then, to me and my mom, "He thinks there's something wrong with his nose."

Big Nick shrugged. "It's a Rocky Balboa nose." He elbowed Paul in the ribs. "A prizefighter nose, right, Paulie?"

"Right, Dad."

"Well," Christina said, "it's a fine nose. I like it."

Watching her lean over and kiss his cheek, I had to hand it to Big Nick. He knows how to break the tension. That is a skill everyone should have—tension-breaking. A skill that can take a person far.

Like now, for instance, when Bob is still hovering six inches behind me, I can turn to him and say, "Are you afraid I might slip?"

"Sorry," he says quietly. He is shuffling his feet, twisting the towel in his hands. I realize what he wants is for me to move, so he can scrub down the coffee bar properly, leaving no germ unwiped.

"That's OK," I say, feeling bad. "You go ahead." I sidestep out of his way so he can do his thing.

I still don't get why Bob is the way he is, but I'm beginning to think he's not any more freakish than the rest of us. Me, my mom, Paul, Big Nick, Christina, Riggs, Liv, Jonathan. We may not be germ-a-phobes, but we all have our peccadilloes, our irrational fears: the fear of falling too hard, or of never falling at all; the fear of screwing up, or of getting screwed; the fear of being held too tight, or of not knowing when to let go.

This morning before school, my mom walked into my room with the box from the attic. Paul's letters. "I think you should have this."

I looked at her carefully. "Why?"

"It's your history," she said. "How it all began."

"It's your history too," I reminded her.

She shook her head. "No."

"Yes, it is, Mom. *You* lived it."

I felt sad, watching her put the box down on my bed. I felt like she should be sad, too, for what she was giving up.

"If you thought you could get him back," I said, "would you try?"

She smiled a little when I said that. Then she shook her head again. "I'm tired of looking backward, Josie. I'm ready to move on."

"With Jonathan?" I said.

"Maybe with Jonathan. Maybe on my own. . . . Maybe in a nunnery somewhere . . . you know, swearing off men forever, until I'm too old and withered to care . . ."

I stared at her.

"Kidding, Josie," she said, laughing. "I'm kidding."

"You'd better be," I said.

The last thing I want to imagine is my mother in a wimple, hunched over a cane. I want her to stay exactly the way she is, with her spiky hair and penchant for cheesy '80s movies, and when people see her coming they say, "Look, there's Josie's mom." They tell me she's a babe, and they're right. They tell me I'm lucky to have her for a mother, and they're right about that, too. For sixteen years she's been the only parent I've ever known—the only one I've needed. I don't know how things will change now, with Paul Tucci in our lives. It remains to be seen, I guess. But I know that whatever happens, my mom will be OK. We both will.

"Josie?" Bob says now, pulling me out of my reverie.

"Yeah?" I say.

"You have a customer."

I turn, and there he is. Matt Rigby, standing at the cookie counter. Smiling that smile. I know he's here to pick me up and drive me home, and yet a part of me still can't believe it.

"Welcome to Fiorello's," I say, sidling my way along the display cases until we're facing each other. "Can I offer you a beverage?"

"Hmm," he says, pretending to think hard. "What do you recommend?"

"A Joseaccino, perhaps? We also have a fine selection of gourmet teas. . . ." I am dorking out, but I don't care. This is Riggs. And with Riggs, I can act however I want. That is the beauty of it.

I know what we have may not last forever. It may not even last the school year. But it's here now. And that is why I don't even wait for him to order; I just lean across the glass and kiss him, square on the mouth. I can only imagine the look on Bob's face right now. But what can I say? I'm a wild and crazy teenager, making out with my boyfriend across the cookie counter, germing up the joint.

ACKNOWLEDGMENTS

Thank you first and foremost to the divine Joy Peskin, whose encouragement after the Night Swimming debacle kept me from taking a long leap off a short pier. Joy's keen eye, her listening ear, and her smiley faces in the margins made her a pleasure to work with.

Thank you to Dr. Kornelia Keszler for keeping the devil Lyme disease at bay so I could write without seeing double.

To the boys of my youth (you know who you are), thanks for the memories, and for the primary source material, from which I borrowed mercilessly to write Paul Tucci's letters.

Huge hugs to Kelsey Nickerson, who shared the minutiae of her soccer team experience (love those rubber bands) and whose diabetes research helped me to create Big Nick.

A shout-out to Party Cake and Rake Face for making me feel Sparky, even when I wasn't.

To George, thank you for embracing you inner teenage girl, and for always wanting to read what I've written.

Love and gratitude to Beebo and G'Ma—grandmothers extraordinaire— and to Daddy Kuj, for manning the troops so I could write, uninterrupted, for more than five seconds.

To Jack and Ben, thank you for making me laugh and for reminding me of what really matters.

Last, but definitely not least, thank you to baby Emma, for having the good sense to arrive AFTER this book was finished.